WORK ME UP

RIGGS BROTHERS, BOOK 3

JULIE KRISS

ISBN: 978-1-989121-02-3

ONE

Ryan

I'D SEEN this movie before. This time the doctor was a woman, the office had a painting of a running horse, and the room smelled a little like menthol. Switch up those three things and you'd have any other appointment I'd had in the last year.

"There is another specialist I can send you to," the sports doctor—Evers, her name was Evers—said as she clicked her laptop. She was about thirty, Asian, and like all of the others, she was entirely competent. "I can forward the scans. He specializes in these kinds of deep tissue problems. You can get an appointment in about eight weeks."

I sat in the chair across from her desk. I'd put my clothes back on—worn-in jeans, Henley, zipped hoodie. I was suddenly so tired I wasn't sure I could get up again. "No," I said.

She blinked in surprise and looked up from her laptop. "No?"

"No," I said again. I didn't even have the energy to sound

mad. "It won't work, and eight weeks is too long. So thank you, but no."

She looked concerned. "Mr. Riggs—"

"Ryan."

"Ryan. I know that this can seem hopeless, even devastating. I know that this is affecting your career. But I think you need to keep trying to find an answer."

An answer to why my right shoulder was messed up, frozen and sliced with pain. An answer to why I couldn't play baseball, which was the only thing that made me money and the only thing I knew how to do. "I've been trying to find an answer for a year," I explained patiently. "It isn't happening."

"It doesn't mean it can't happen." God, these doctors—especially the high-paid sports ones—were so fucking smooth. Just the right words, just the right tone. Maybe it was experience with dealing with egotistical assholes like me. "The only way to guarantee you won't play again is to give up."

"Nice," I said. "I saw that on the wall somewhere. Was that in this office or the last one?"

"What?"

"Never mind. Do I win something if I give up? Where do I sign?"

She sighed, as if she heard this kind of pathetic shit every day. Like I say, athletes are egotistical assholes. Except in order to have a big ego, you have to have made it big in the first place. I never did—I only ever hit the minor leagues. Now I was twenty-seven, the MLB didn't know I was alive, and my shoulder was toast, though Dr. Evers wouldn't admit it. Hence the pathetic shit.

"This isn't over," she said. "Be persistent. Do the exercises every day. Keep up the stretches and the good diet. Add in as much strength training as you can handle. Sometimes these things just take time. We'll book more scans, and I'll put in for an appointment. He might have an earlier cancellation—you never know."

I have this thing I do in the middle of a game, when I'm on the mound and the pressure gets high: I clock out. I go somewhere else and I watch it like it's a movie, like it's not really me. I did that now, though Dr. Evers didn't notice. I nodded and said thank you and took the slip for the appointment for another scan. I signed the papers for the insurance company and I even flirted with the halfway pretty receptionist, watching her smile. I smiled back and said something witty, and I walked out of the office to my SUV, looking at the vivid blue June sky of Detroit.

When you were an athlete in need of a doctor, it was good to be in the city of the Tigers, the Redwings, and the Pistons. I'd never make it to the Tigers, but at least I could see their doctors if I was willing to pay and to wait for eight weeks.

It felt better, being outside. I always hated being cooped up; it was one of the reasons I'd signed up for baseball when I was thirteen. Back then I was almost flunking school and I had to steal the money for a glove, but when I stood on the field under the sunshine for the first time I didn't want to leave. I sure as hell didn't want to go home, where my mother was long gone, my dad didn't give a shit, and my brothers and I ran wild. When I stood in the baseball field in the sunshine I was just me, and everyone left me the hell alone. Then I threw my first pitch, and everything that happened from that moment led in a straight line to this one.

So even in a concrete parking lot in Detroit I just stood there for a second, soaking it up. There was a jagged throb of pain from my right shoulder down to the middle of my back, brought on by the therapy session, but I was used to that. I pulled a small tube of pills from the pocket of my jeans and popped two, swallowing them dry. They were unlabeled and I was damn sure I wasn't supposed to have them. But an athlete who wants to get his hands on something unlabeled that will make the pain float away always can.

I justified it by telling myself I didn't take them all the time. Just now and then, when the pain was bad.

Except if I was honest, I was taking them all the time.

The only way to guarantee you won't play again is to give up.

Interesting.

I had not, in fact, played baseball in thirteen months. I'd come off a six-game suspension for punching another player in the face —maybe not my finest moment—and played a single game, blistering pitch after pitch off the mound until they benched me in the sixth inning to rest. By then we'd pretty much already won, and I could barely lift my arm. I had slices of pain moving from the center of my shoulder down my back, down my arm, shooting up my neck. I felt like I was made of pain, but we won. I hadn't played since.

There had been workouts, therapy, training. Little white pills. Except for the shoulder I was actually in some of the best shape of my life. I ran five miles a day, I could do situps until I puked and pushups until my shoulder screamed. The only thing I couldn't do was pitch a damn ball.

There were therapy sessions of the mental kind, too—the team had put me in an anger management program, a request from the league that they'd agreed to in order to buy me time. *Get your shit back in shape* was the message I'd gotten, loud and clear. *Now or never, Riggs.*

And now, another doctor. Another eight weeks.

It wasn't just my pride or my ego that were going down the shitter. It was my income. And the problem was, I didn't have just myself to worry about.

My phone rang in my back pocket. I pulled it out. Amanda, the wife of one of my fellow players. I answered it. "What's up?"

"Ryan, it's two o'clock," she said.

I squinted into the distance. I knew that voice from Amanda —it meant I was forgetting something. "Yeah?"

"And you have an appointment at three."

Oh. Right.

"Fuck," I said.

"You promised." Her voice went dark with threat. Amanda was the nicest woman alive—on the surface. But she was one of those women: cross her at your own peril. It came from having a baseball player for a husband. Athletes' wives, the ones who actually make it work, are fierce. My friend Wes, who was married to Amanda, had learned early to do anything she said, no questions asked.

"I did promise," I said. "I'll do it. I'll be there. I have to go pick up Dylan from school, and we're going straight home."

"You forgot, didn't you?"

I wasn't going to answer that. I had forgotten, sort of. Mostly I'd just blocked from my mind that Amanda thought I needed a nanny for my son, and that she believed she'd found just the right person. I'd hoped against hope that she would forget about it—she had two kids of her own and was insanely busy—but I should have known better.

"This is going to work out, I promise," she was saying to me now.

"You really vouch for her? This is my kid we're talking about."

"Ryan, she's my cousin. I've known her since birth. Yes, I vouch for her."

"But she hasn't worked as a nanny before." This part, I remembered.

"She's very qualified. I'd even say *eminently* qualified."

"What does that even mean?"

"It means just meet her. Ryan, you need someone. You need help."

I closed my eyes briefly, because that stung. The truth always did. She was right, I was a fucking mess. I was trying to be a father to a seven-year-old, and even I could see I was failing. "What's her name again?"

"Jesus, Ryan. You'd forget your dick if it wasn't attached to you."

"No. No, I would not." Really.

"Her name is Kate," Amanda said. "Kate. *Kate.* K-A-T-E."

"Okay, okay." Kate. That twigged something in my memory. "Have I met her?"

"I don't think so. She doesn't travel in baseball circles. She doesn't like baseball at all, actually."

That was a strike in her favor. The pills were starting to kick in now, the world receding. "Fine. I'll talk to her."

"Talk to her, then hire her."

Amanda was nice and all, but she continually reminded me why I didn't get married. "Yes, ma'am." *Though I have no idea with what money.*

"I'm right, you'll see," she said. "I'll talk to you later."

TWO

Ryan

MY SEVEN-YEAR-OLD SON, Dylan, was waiting in the school doorway when I pulled up. They kept the kids inside the school when the parents were late, because they didn't want the kids running free for creeps to pick up. Honest to God, this was parenting. From the day I learned to walk my father barely knew where I was, and yet I spent every day freaked the hell out, looking in the bushes for crazies.

I was only fifteen minutes late, but that was a fuckup, of course. Because in those fifteen minutes, someone could have snatched and killed my kid. He came out the door when he saw my car, hefting his backpack. Was he too skinny? I tried to feed him as much as I could. His jeans were two inches too long, and he'd rolled them up. If some kid at school gave him grief for having rolled-up pants, I'd wreak vengeance.

Until three years ago, when Dylan showed up unexpectedly

on my doorstep at the age of four, I'd been carefree Ryan Riggs, the guy who pitched ball and fucked any girl he wanted. I hadn't cared about a single thing. Now, I was certifiably insane.

"Hey, Dad," Dylan said as he got in the passenger seat.

"Sorry I'm late." I'd apologized more in the last three years than I ever had in my life.

Dylan shrugged and pulled his seatbelt on.

"I forgot to tell you something," I said as I pulled away. "We're meeting someone back home right now. A woman."

"You have a girlfriend?" He looked stricken, as if I'd told him to get out of the car and find somewhere else to live. My son was easygoing considering all of the changes in his short life, but the one thing that made him panic was the idea of me having a girl-friend. Maybe he thought a girlfriend would take me away from him, and I was the only parent he knew.

I hadn't even had a date since he came to live with me, let alone screwed anyone or started a relationship. But Dylan had a thing about it, and every time it crossed his anxious seven-year-old mind, he looked like he was going to puke.

"No, dude, I don't have a girlfriend." I'd learned that the secret was to sound casual, make a joke of it. That always unwound him. "Come on. Who would date me?"

"Mrs. Thorold," he said instantly.

I had no idea who that was. A teacher? I was pretty sure I'd met them all at the parent-teacher thing. "Mrs. Thorold sounds married," I said easily. "That isn't cool. Anyway, this woman isn't a girlfriend. She's a nanny. Or she will be if we decide to hire her."

He thought about this hard for a second. "What does a nanny do?"

"Help you get ready for school. Pick you up when I have appointments. Make your lunches. That kind of thing."

"I make my own lunches."

I'd tried. I really had. But when I packed Dylan's lunch, he didn't eat it. It was only after I'd let him start packing it himself that he actually ate lunch every day. He didn't pack himself junk, either—he just wanted his sandwich a certain way that I couldn't imitate, apparently. "Well, she'll help you with that, so you don't have to do as much."

"Will she take me to baseball practice?"

He'd started baseball this year, and he loved it. Getting him to practice was always a stretch. "Yeah, she'll do that, and make sure you have your equipment."

"Don't you want to do that?"

Jeez, kid, rip my heart out, why don't you? "I do, but I have to go make a living, so sometimes she'll help out when I'm not around. We're meeting her this afternoon, and we're going to talk to her. If we like her, we'll hire her."

"What if we don't like her?"

"Then we won't hire her."

"Okay." He looked out the window, then started talking about something he'd learned in geography class. He seemed to be done with it. Score one for me.

Ryan Riggs, world's number one father.

This was going to go just fine.

———

SHE RANG the doorbell thirty minutes after we got home. Dylan had gotten himself a snack—crackers and peanut butter, because the world's number one father didn't have junk food in the house—and was sitting at the kitchen table with his tablet, playing a game. I didn't trust the tablet further than I could throw it with my barely functional throwing arm, but I was learning to live with it. Dylan liked it, and he was a responsible kid. I'd learned to access and use the thing so I could make sure there were no creepers there either.

If I'd ever mentioned perverts or serial killers to my father, he would have laughed in my face. *Just run, you pussy, and hope you're fast.* My father's life advice to me and my three brothers was always punctuated by *you pussy*. That was my one and only lesson in fatherhood: Try not to be Dad.

I walked to the door, thinking that maybe the house was a mess. We tried to be clean, but we were two guys living here, and things got messy. Maybe she wouldn't want to work for us anyway. If that happened, I'd just tell Amanda to find me someone else. Because I was starting to believe she was right: I could improve things for Dylan, money be damned, if I had some help.

It just had to be the right woman.

I opened the door and a woman stood there. In her twenties, a redhead with her hair tied back in a wavy ponytail. She was wearing jeans, a gray T-shirt with a black cardigan over it, low-heeled boots. She was wearing big sunglasses, and she took them off and looked at me. She was hot in an understated way—curves packed into those jeans, more curves tucked under the cardigan, big dark eyes and a nice mouth. The problem wasn't that she was hot. The problem was I recognized her.

Kate. The name. Now I knew where I remembered it from. I'd met a Kate before.

I knew this woman. I knew her face and I knew every inch of her body, every curve. She looked at me and I knew she knew me, too.

"Jesus," I said.

"Yeah," Kate said. "I know. We slept together five years ago."

THREE

Kate

HERE'S the first thing you need to know about Ryan Riggs: He's gorgeous. Utterly, perfectly gorgeous, from his handsome face all the way down his lickable body. Seeing him for the first time is like taking a hit of helium or laughing gas. Your head goes light and your skin goes hot and you have to bite your tongue, because whatever comes out of your mouth is either going to be verbal nonsense or a high-pitched giggle. I've met good-looking men before, but Ryan Riggs is a man who will make you legitimately stupid.

It's almost ridiculous, how good-looking he is. Who actually looks like that? He has the kind of looks that make otherwise smart women do very, very stupid things. I knew because I was a smart woman who had done exactly one crazy, risky, stupid thing in her life, and that thing was with Ryan Riggs after a party five years ago.

Well, technically I did that crazy thing with him three times. In one night.

I had never done anything like it, before or since. It was my one night of rebellion.

It was even better than you think it was.

My cousin Amanda, of course, had no idea. She thought I was the smart, straight-A cousin she'd always known, not a woman who would throw herself at a baseball player—three times—when she didn't even know the first thing about baseball. No, that was something Kate Washington would never do, and I wasn't about to enlighten her. So when Amanda had suggested I apply for the nanny job for her husband's friend Ryan, a baseball player who needed help with his son, I had no excuse to say no. *Sorry, I jumped into bed with him one crazy night five years ago and I can still remember every raw second of it, so I think that would be awkward.*

It wasn't that I was ashamed. I was single, and I'm well aware of what year it is. It's just that you don't necessarily tell your cousin these things so that she can stare at you funny every Christmas for the rest of your life.

Even crazier than the fact that I had done it was the fact that it had been good. Good for the usual physical, orgasmic reasons— but also good for my mind. That night had built my confidence, made me think I could do more than I thought I could. Which was why I had really, truly hoped never to see Ryan again. Which makes no sense. There were very good reasons I didn't have a boyfriend.

And still, when Amanda had suggested I apply for the job with Ryan, I'd said yes. That's the Ryan Riggs effect.

I'd hoped that five years might make him fat and bald, but I should have known better. He was still tall and dark-haired and clean-shaven and freakishly hot. He was wearing jeans and a tee with a hoodie thrown over it, worn open. Bare feet. Tousled hair.

Dark eyes, flawless high cheekbones. Even the hand braced against the doorframe was masculine and perfectly formed, the bones of the long fingers and the tendons of the wrist like works of art. *It is completely incredible that a man who looks like this ever slept with you,* a voice in my head said. *How the hell did that happen?*

I had no idea. He recognized me, and he was looking at me with an expression that was narrowed and almost wary, like he suspected some kind of scam.

"*You're* Amanda's cousin?" he asked.

I nodded. "The party we met at—it was Amanda and Wes who were actually invited. They were supposed to go, but they couldn't. They gave me their invitation instead."

It had been a party for baseball players, of all people. A benefit. I did not watch baseball or any other sport. I wasn't even sure I knew the rules. (Hit the ball, run around the bases? Right?) But I'd been in my third year of college, and I felt like I'd done nothing but study all my life. I was tired of being clever, brainy, straight-A Kate all the time. Something had come over me, and on impulse I'd decided to be someone else for one night.

And I had.

"Huh," Ryan said, leaning on the doorframe, his gaze going up and down me, taking me in. "You didn't say you were a nanny."

"I wasn't," I said, narrowing my eyes back at him. "And speaking of not saying, you never mentioned a kid."

He stared me down, calculating. Amanda said the son was seven. A kid meant a woman, at least in a lot of cases.

"You think I was cheating?" he said.

"Were you?"

"She had the kid and didn't tell me. We weren't together. We aren't. I only got Dylan a few years ago. Are we straight?"

Reluctantly, I nodded. There was obviously more to the story

—like what the words *I got Dylan* meant—but Amanda and Wes wouldn't vouch for a man who was a dirtbag cheater. And they had vouched for Ryan.

He's a good guy. You'll like him, Wes had said. *His career is in the shitter right now, but it isn't his fault. Riggs just has bad luck.*

He has a bad reputation, Amanda had said, *but ignore that. It's just people talking. Ryan is a good person. He just doesn't think before he acts sometimes.*

There was something about a shoulder injury, and I realized too late that I should have Googled him, because he didn't look injured. He just looked like the badass, foxy baseball player who had picked me up and taken me home five years ago. And I'd let myself get picked up and taken. It could have ended up awkward and bad but oh my God, it hadn't.

"You sure you want to do this?" he asked me now.

Right. Work for him. I shrugged, trying to look casual. Looking at him was like looking directly at the sun, so I directed my gaze to a spot on the doorframe. "Amanda says you need help. I see no reason why we can't make it work."

He seemed to consider that. "Okay," he said. "Come in."

I followed him into the house and down the hall. It truly isn't a hardship to follow Ryan Riggs anywhere—he has a way of walking that's sort of stupefying, his shoulders back and casual, his hips sinuous, his long athlete's legs and his perfect ass in motion. They could make a TV show called *Ryan Riggs Walks Around*, and women would tune in every week. *This week: Ryan walks around a supermarket. Next week: Ryan walks around a park.* It was a million-dollar idea.

His house was a small bungalow, cluttered with mess: toys and a kid's schoolbooks, baseball gear, wide-open video game boxes, boots and shoes and jackets. The décor was simple, in that it was basically rooms with furniture in them. That was it. This was definitely a house with no woman in it.

We entered the kitchen where a boy sat at the table, eating crackers and poking at a tablet. He was wearing a baggy tee and a baseball cap, and he looked up at me with sweet, intelligent eyes. "Hi," he said.

"Hi," I said, holding out my hand. "I'm Kate."

"I'm Dylan," he said, and shook it. This boy had basically won the gene pool, and it showed. He didn't look exactly like Ryan—he was fairer, his eyes and hair lighter—but he had a perfect, beautiful little face. At the moment it was very adult and serious-looking, probably because his father had told him about this interview. I didn't have kids, and I'd never had a particular jones for them, but it was impossible not to like this one. I wondered where his mother was.

Ryan pulled out a chair at the table next to his son and sat down. He motioned for me to do the same. I assumed we'd start with some small talk and basics, but instead Ryan said, "Dylan, say something to impress Kate."

"Pi is three point one four," Dylan said immediately. "It's been calculated past a trillion digits."

Ryan jerked a thumb at Dylan. "Can you believe he's seven? I was failing school at his age."

"It isn't that hard, Dad," Dylan said. "They tell you everything in class."

"Yeah, well, I didn't go all that often," Ryan said. "That's why you're smarter than me." He looked at me. "Do you want anything? We might have some coffee somewhere."

"I'm fine," I said.

Ryan sat back in his chair. "Okay, I'll get down to business. I'm not gonna lie. I need a nanny for this kid."

Dylan perked up at that. "Dad says you can take me to baseball practice."

"Um, yes," I said. "I can do that."

Ryan ran a hand through his hair. "The thing is, I have

therapy and appointments and stuff. I'm sort of bad with routine."

"Dad's always late," Dylan supplied, though there was no anger in his tone.

Ryan just nodded, like he copped to it. "Okay, I'm not on time a lot. Dylan needs to get to school and back. And to baseball practice on Wednesdays. And when school is out I need help over the summer." He scratched his chin. "He has day camp and stuff. Birthday parties. He needs his lunch made every day, because he doesn't like how I make it."

"I can make it," Dylan said. He turned to me magnanimously and added, "You can help."

When Amanda had used the word *nanny*, I'd pictured babies or toddlers. I'd forgotten that Dylan was seven. Making a few sandwiches and driving this boy around didn't seem as hard as I'd thought. "That sounds fine," I said.

"Amanda says you're qualified," Ryan said, and my good feelings vanished.

Shit.

I cleared my throat. "Well, I, um—I'm college educated."

His eyebrows rose. "I didn't know that," he said, and what he meant was *You didn't mention it five years ago when I took you home and banged you senseless.*

"No," I said. "I didn't mention it." Which meant *I didn't want to be a serious college student that night five years ago, I wanted to have some mindless hot sex instead.*

"Right," Ryan said, as if I'd spoken out loud. "What are you educated in?"

I put my hands in my lap. "I have an English degree."

"Can you help with my English homework?" Dylan asked. "I have to know what nouns and verbs are."

"Yes, I can help you with that," I said, trying not to smile.

Ryan's gorgeous eyes were fixed on me. "But you're not a teacher," he said.

"No," I said, and for a crazy second I had the urge to lie—to say whatever it took to get this job, to stay in this place with this man. I swallowed down the impulse and told him the truth instead. "I've never worked as a nanny before," I said, holding his gaze. "To tell you the truth, I got my college degree and I haven't done anything with it. Right now I'm working as a pet sitter."

There was a long, uncomfortable silence.

Ryan and Dylan looked at each other. "A pet sitter?" Ryan said.

"I was an office manager before that," I said. "And before that, I worked at a florist's. I guess you could say I've been at loose ends, professionally, since I finished college." *Which was four years ago, much to my parents' dismay.*

Ryan lowered his chin, his deep brown eyes fixed on me. "Amanda used the words *eminently qualified.*"

I rubbed a hand over my face. "She meant that I'm responsible and trustworthy. And I am. I'm good with details and I'm always on time." I dropped my hand. "And I'll work for a discount."

That made Ryan's eyebrows go up again. "A discount? You want a job that bad?"

"To make up for the fact that I have no experience. That you're taking a chance on me."

"I don't know." Ryan glanced at his son. "Dylan is pretty easy to take care of. Put some food out for him, take him for the odd walk, and he's fine."

"Dad!" Dylan said.

But my gaze locked on Ryan's, and for a second it was just the two of us in the room. "It's up to you," I said to him. "Honestly."

He looked thoughtful, still holding my gaze. "How far away

are you?" he asked me. "Are you still in that place on Chester Street?"

Right. He knew where I lived five years ago, because he'd taken me home there. And he'd fucked me in my bed there, and he'd made me come three times before he left. "Um, no," I said, feeling my cheeks burn for the first time in this little encounter. "I don't live there anymore. I live on Montgomery Avenue now."

"Not far," Ryan said.

I shook my head. I didn't tell him that I lived with roommates now, because pet sitter income didn't allow for an apartment to myself. I had a little money from my parents, but I was trying to live without it and go it on my own. Trying, and not really succeeding. I had already dipped into my parents' fund for me more times than I wanted to count. And if I worked for Ryan at a discount, I'd do it again.

There was another long silence, punctuated by a crunch as Dylan ate a cracker and went back to his iPad.

"Dylan?" Ryan said finally. "You're the one who has to spend time with her. What do you think?"

"I like her," Dylan said.

Ryan smiled. It was deadly, that smile. It was the kind of smile that melted knees and made panties vanish. Not that mine would. That had been a one-time thing.

"Okay," Ryan said. "You're hired, Kate the college graduate pet sitter. Think it over. If you want the job, you start in the morning."

FOUR

Ryan

A COLLEGE STUDENT. She'd been a fucking college student five years ago, and now she was a college grad. She was class, too, I could see that now. She was smart and responsible, like Amanda said. And she could afford to work for me for next to nothing, which meant she probably came from money.

In short, she was way, way above my league.

I hadn't known that on that first night. That first night, she'd worn a sexy black dress on her curves, and she'd seemed sweet and maybe a little bit nervous. She was hot and she smelled good. I wanted to make her laugh, to make her feel less nervous, and then I wanted to get her naked and make her come. And I always got what I wanted.

She was that same woman now, but not exactly. She had grown her hair longer and put it in a soft ponytail with stray pieces curling against the side of her neck. She was more poised—the nervousness was completely gone—and she was harder to impress. She made working as a pet sitter look classy, like something everyone should aspire to. Like it was a perfectly natural career. I couldn't pull off being a fucking baseball player, but she could pull off being a pet sitter like she was in a magazine.

But as far as hotness went, she was the same woman. Better. Because now I wanted to crack her dignified shell, strip her naked, make her beg, and *then* make her come. In that order.

There was a reason they called me the Bad Boy of Baseball.

As soon as the door closed behind her, I sent Dylan to do homework in his room where he couldn't hear. Then I called Wes. My friend Wes, husband of Amanda, who had sent the Ghost of One-Night Stands to my doorstep to work as my nanny.

"Tell me you liked her," Wes said when he answered. He was outdoors somewhere, with wind blowing into the speaker. "If you didn't, you're an idiot."

"I want her to work for me, but she hasn't decided," I said. "What do I do?"

He whistled. "That's a tough one. Kate is smart and independent. She makes her own decisions."

I looked in the fridge, trying to think of something to have for dinner. As with every other day, I had no fucking idea. "She's willing to work for peanuts, so it isn't money she's after." Not that I had any. "How do I sweeten the deal?"

"You think I know the answer to that?"

"I need intel. Whatever you have."

"Hmm." He took his sweet time, which made me want to smack his teeth in. "Kate is brainy. Really brainy. But she's been sort of directionless since college. Her parents are Amanda's aunt and uncle. They have tons of money, and Kate is their only child. They're disappointed in her."

"Why? Because she didn't make some big career yet?"

"It's important to them. Amanda adores Kate, but to be honest she's sort of the black sheep the family right now."

I smiled to myself. This, I could work with. "What else? Does she have a boyfriend?"

"There was a serious guy that her parents wanted her to marry, but she didn't. Part of the reason why her parents are mad."

Bingo. "And no boyfriends since?"

Wes paused. "Wait a second, Riggs. Why are you asking?"

I reached into the fridge and picked up a tomato. Could we have tomato sandwiches for dinner? Was that starving my kid or something? "Intel, I told you."

"No way. I know you, Riggs. You're a player."

"Correction. I *was* a player. Now I'm a single dad, and I'm completely fucking celibate." It wasn't even a lie, which was something that made me want to jump off a cliff on a regular basis. "I'm just trying to figure out where Kate's head is at. If there's some guy who's going to be pissed if she works for me."

"If you're celibate and your intentions are pure, then why would some guy be pissed that she's working for you?"

I tossed the tomato in the air and caught it. Maybe I should try pitching a tomato and see if my arm improved. "Because I'm very, very fucking good-looking," I told Wes. "I know you're straight and all, but are you blind?"

Wes sighed. "I don't even know why I'm friends with you."

"I know," I said. "I have everything I need, thanks."

I hung up on him and dug some non-moldy bread out of the bread bin. Tomato sandwiches it was. I found some cheese in the fridge, and then, worried about nutrition, I grabbed the box of bran cereal. Tomato sandwiches *and* cereal. Ryan Riggs, world's number one father.

Kate Washington was a straight arrow. A brainy college girl. Except I knew something no one else knew: she'd spent a night with me, the Bad Boy of Baseball, a man she'd just met. It had been very, very fucking hot. Like steam-the-windows hot. And she didn't tell me about college or anything else, because that night she was rebelling.

She might be doing it in a quieter way five years later, but she was still rebelling. Making her parents mad.

I already had two things going for me: sex and rebellion. I was excellent at both.

I had my answer. Kate was going to be my nanny.

And I wasn't going to have to do a damn thing.

FIVE

Kate

THERE WAS no way I could be Ryan's nanny. Absolutely
no way.

It hit me as I was driving home, once the fog of estrogen and
pure lust wore off. I gripped the wheel and made the list in
my head.

Reasons Why I Cannot Be Ryan Riggs' Nanny:

We have a history.

I keep picturing him naked.

It was spectacular.

I want to sleep with him.

This will end badly.

That was it.

It really came down to one thing: Ryan was trouble. For most
of womankind, really. But specifically for me.

He hadn't seemed like trouble five years ago. He'd been

charming and funny and hot. We'd met at a charity benefit, and he was wearing a suit—my knuckles went white on the wheel, just remembering Ryan in a suit. I'd been standing at the bar, waiting for the bartender to notice me and wondering if I would talk to anyone at all that night—it seemed unlikely—and a man stepped up beside me, waiting too. I glanced at him and he glanced back, and we both froze.

It was a weird, electric moment. A thought popped into my head: *There's no way this guy will talk to me.* But when the moment went on a little too long, he said, "I like your lip gloss."

And from nowhere, I flirted like a pro. "Is that a come-on?" I asked him.

The corner of his gorgeous mouth curled. "Is it really that easy?"

"You could at least buy me a drink," I said.

He tapped a finger on the bar, like he was thinking it over. "It's an open bar, so you have a deal," he said. "By the way, my name is Ryan Riggs."

We talked. He was funny and drop-dead gorgeous, but he also had a rough edge to him that made my girl parts go crazy. When I told him I knew nothing about baseball, his reply was *I honestly don't give a shit.* When I asked if he had a girlfriend, he said *Are you out of your fucking mind?* Direct and raunchy. A man who could wear a suit, but wasn't born in one. I had just broken up with the man my parents wanted me to marry, and this baseball player of all people—sexy, uneducated but street-smart, an athlete who inhabited his body and used it to its fullest every day—was suddenly, exactly what I needed.

And he wanted to sleep with me. *With me.* Kate Washington, who normally would have spent this evening wearing glasses and plaid pajama pants, studying for exams that were three weeks away. He didn't talk to anyone else that night, though there were plenty of people milling around. Only me. He made me feel sexy and special and beautiful, and when he said *Let me drive you home* I said yes. It was so easy.

And oh my god, the sex.

I was not thinking about it. I really was not.

I pulled into the parking lot of my apartment building and turned off the car, slumping in my seat.

The first time, he'd used his mouth and I'd come so fast it was almost embarrassing. But the second time... oh Jesus, the second time. And then the third time—

Stop it, Kate.

I hadn't had sex like that before. I hadn't known you *could* have sex like that. I'd had sex exactly two times in the last five years, and both had been letdowns compared to Ryan, which I wasn't going to admit to him.

But a man like that probably had women beating his door down. If I worked for him, would I be babysitting Dylan while Ryan went on dates? Because I didn't think I could handle that.

Another Reason I Cannot Be Ryan Riggs' Nanny: watching him date women who aren't me.

Would I have to meet the women coming out his bedroom in the morning? The thought made me ill. I picked up my purse and got out of the car.

In my apartment, my roommate Tessa was in the living room watching TV with her boyfriend, and my other roommate, Melanie, was in the kitchen making an egg sandwich. Because I was twenty-six and I lived with roommates. Everything was fine.

"I got a new job," I said to the room in general as I toed my shoes off. There was no point directing your conversation to an individual in my apartment since everyone could hear everything anyways.

Tessa barely glanced at me and Melanie raised her eyebrows. Tessa's boyfriend—I had no idea what his name was—didn't even look my way.

"Where?" Melanie asked.

"Working for a baseball player, taking care of his son."

That made the boyfriend briefly perk up. "One of the Tigers?"

"No. His name is Ryan Riggs."

The boyfriend's eyebrows shot up higher than Melanie's had. "No shit?"

Well, damn. I'd just impressed a man with sports for the first time in my life. Maybe I could use this on the next date I went on. "Yes. I start tomorrow." *As long as I take the job.*

The boyfriend still looked amazed, and Melanie had pulled out her phone and Googled his picture. "Holy shit, girl. Is he single?"

I narrowed my eyes at her, though she wasn't looking. Melanie was single like me, except she was the size of a toothpick. "I think he's off the market, actually."

"Really?" Melanie used her thumb and finger to enlarge the photo she was looking at on her phone. "He must have a girl-friend. He does *not* look gay."

"He can't be gay if he has a kid," Tessa piped up from the sofa.

"Duh, sure he can," Melanie said.

"Riggs isn't gay, man," the boyfriend proclaimed. "He punched a guy on the field last year and got suspended. It was fucking badass."

"He *punched* someone?" I said. Amanda hadn't told me that, just alluded to acting without thinking. *Riggs just has bad luck,* Wes had said. Punching someone didn't sound like bad luck.

"Boom," the boyfriend, said, miming it. "Blood all over the guy's uniform. A spray coming out of his nose. It's on YouTube. Check it out, it's amazing."

I hadn't Googled Ryan five years ago, but it was time. I

poured a glass of wine first, then retreated to my room. I didn't think my phone was going to cut it, so I opened my laptop.

The first thing that came up under his name was a page with the article *Ryan Riggs: The Bad Boy of Baseball*. Oh no. I drank some wine and kept scrolling.

Riggs suspended for on-field assault

Opinion: Players like Ryan Riggs bring down the sport

"He just hit me," Harding says of Riggs

League enrolls Riggs in anger management training during suspension

Will the league allow Riggs back on the field?

What is the future of Ryan Riggs?

After six-game suspension, Riggs pitches perfect

Shoulder injury puts Riggs in the dugout

Riggs will be out the rest of the season, doctors say

Will Riggs come back to the field? And if he does, what shape will he be in?

Riggs has no comment about the shoulder injury keeping him in the dugout for another season

I clicked on the video of the punch. There was Ryan in uniform on the field. What was it about baseball pants? Seeing him wearing them almost made me want to watch the sport.

Another player was talking to Ryan, gesturing and pointing, maybe giving some kind of strategy. Ryan stood and listened, his fingers hooked on his hipbones, a casual stance that showed off his gorgeous frame. He looked at the other man for a second, like he was just noticing he was there—and then his arm shot out and the other player's head snapped back. *Boom!* Just like Tessa's boyfriend had said. I clapped my hand over my mouth.

The headline below the video said, *The Bad Boy of Baseball throws a punch on the mound!*

I dragged the cursor back and watched the video again. Ryan didn't look mad; he wasn't shouting or even arguing. He was just listening, and then he was giving the other player a nosebleed. If you could keep from wincing, it was almost funny—almost. Because he looked totally cool while he did it. He certainly didn't look like a man who needed anger management classes.

Sitting at my little desk, I leaned my forehead on my hand. What was I getting into? I was a straight-A English major college grad. He was the Bad Boy of Baseball. We didn't belong on the same planet.

And yet... that night five years ago, we *had* belonged on the same planet. In the same bed, in fact. It didn't make sense, but it was there. Alone in my room, sipping my wine, I could admit that maybe, in some corner of my mind, I had a thing for bad boys. Ryan was a disaster, and something about that turned me on.

I looked at the video on my screen. To be honest, it made me a little hot. It was the way he moved, the way he simply didn't give a shit what anyone thought. It was horrifying and sexy at the same time.

I picked up my phone and called Ryan's number.

He answered on the second ring, his voice low like he was half asleep. "Yeah?"

"It's Kate."

"I know."

I took a breath. "I'll take the job," I said.

"Yeah?" He sounded almost like he'd expected it, damn him.

"Yes. But I think I should warn you. I'm not really the motherly type."

"Okay." He seemed confused.

"I'm just saying I'm not Mary Poppins, but I'll do my best. Also, I have a few ground rules."

"Like what?"

"Like no sex."

There was a brief pause. "Between us, or with other people?"

My jaw dropped. I almost barked it: *No sex with other people. At least for you.* Instead I said, "Between us, of course."

He was quiet for a long second. Then his voice came, low and a little frustrated. "You ask a lot of a guy."

Something deep between my legs melted like hot wax. *Stay strong, Kate.* "I think you can handle it, Ryan."

He sighed, put-upon. "Okay, I agree."

"Good. Also, I don't do housework. No dishes, no laundry, and I don't take the garbage out."

"I'm not hiring a fucking maid, Kate."

"No, but I've seen that house. It's Testosterone Central. I'm not cleaning it."

Now he sounded annoyed. "Kate, do not clean my house. I like my testosterone where it is. I won't try to jump you. And where did you get this shit about being motherly? Can you make sure my kid gets to school and back without a serial killer getting him?"

"Yes. Yes, I can do that."

"Then you're hired," he said, and hung up.

I stared at my blank phone screen. I was going to need a lot more wine.

Ryan Riggs. Hottie, athlete, single dad, one-night stand, face puncher, definitely not gay, and apparently badass.

And as of tomorrow, my new boss.

This was going to go just fine.

SIX

Kate

Week One

WHERE IS HE? I wondered as I laid out the Snakes and Ladders game board on the kitchen table. I had picked Dylan up from school over three hours ago and there was no sign of Ryan. We had gone to the park and I'd looked at Dylan's homework. He wanted spaghetti for dinner, so I made it while he helped me, standing on a stool at the kitchen counter. Now we each had a bowl of spaghetti and we were going to play a game while we ate.

I was still getting used to this kid—to any kid. Dylan wasn't much trouble so far, but he had his personality quirks: he liked to make or at least oversee his own food, he never knew where his backpack was, he wanted to wear the same *Star Wars* shirt every day. He was trying to behave nicely for me this first week—it was cute and kind of heartbreaking—but I could tell he had an energetic and goofy side. He thought mushrooms were gross and his father was God. I wondered where his mother was.

He wanted to play the game at the kitchen table while we ate. Maybe this wasn't something you were supposed to let a kid do, but I didn't really know, and it sounded harmless to me. If Ryan had a problem with it, I'd remind him once again that I wasn't Mary Poppins. Actually, if Ryan had a problem with it he could stuff it, because he wasn't even home.

We were on our second game—it turned out that the rules of Snakes and Ladders were whatever Dylan said they were, which of course meant he was winning—when the front door opened and Ryan came home. He walked into the kitchen, wearing low-slung jeans and a navy blue Henley that fit him like a second skin. His hair was damp and mussed, like he'd just gotten out of the shower. He leaned a shoulder on the doorjamb and looked past his son to me.

"He suckered you into Snakes and Ladders, I see," he said. "I learned my lesson a long time ago."

"Dad, I'm winning," Dylan said.

"Of course you are," Ryan replied. "Is that spaghetti?"

Dylan picked up the dice. "We made it. Where were you?"

Ryan rubbed a hand over his face, and for a second I saw his expression go hard, like he was in pain. Then he erased it and relaxed his face again. "Doctor's appointment, and then the gym." He frowned. "Oh, shit. I forgot to pick something up on the way home, didn't I?"

"Bread," Dylan said, studying the board.

"Shit," Ryan said again.

Here was Ryan Riggs as a father: he swore in front of his seven-year-old son, he was late all the time, he never cooked, and Dylan *still* thought he was God. In the past week I'd been showered with Ryan's baseball stats, his strikeouts and walks and hits per inning. Or something. I had no idea what Dylan was talking about, but he knew all the numbers.

Now Ryan fixed his gaze on me. His voice was soft when he spoke. "He okay?"

I swallowed. It was best, I'd decided, if I simply acted professional in this job. Like there was nothing in the past to think about. No sir. I tucked a lock of stray hair behind my ear. "He's fine," I answered him. "He's good."

"Thanks for staying," Ryan said. "I'm sorry we kept you. You can go if you have plans."

I felt my face get hot. "No problem. I don't have plans."

Our eyes locked. Ryan's expression went dark, intent. Between us, Dylan rolled the dice and moved his marker around —probably up another ladder—and I didn't pay attention, because I was staring at the man in the doorway. My God, he could really fucking *smolder*. I could almost smell smoke in the air.

"You sure?" he said, his voice a little rough. "No plans?"

"Ryan," I managed.

"Dad." Dylan interrupted us, turning in his chair, oblivious to the dirty thoughts that had just been going through my head. "Can we go for ice cream?"

Ryan tore his gaze from mine and frowned at Dylan. "Ice cream? Do you see this?" He lifted the hem of his shirt, showing his bare stomach. "I just came from the gym. You don't get this by having ice cream on a school night."

I stared, transfixed. All those abs, slabs of tight muscle locked together. The V muscles over his hips, disappearing into his jeans. The line of dark hair that made his happy trail. I had traveled that happy trail. I had gone all the way down. Down, down...

I lifted my gaze to Ryan's. He was watching me—he knew exactly what he was doing, the bastard. It was all for show.

His expression, though, was a mixture of humor and dead seriousness. The question was clear: *You like it?*

I schooled my face to look bored, even though it was too little, too late. "Do you need abs to throw a ball?" I asked.

"Sure you do," Ryan said, dropping his shirt. It took an effort on my part not to groan. "You need them to run, too."

"I thought you just stood on the pitcher's mound for the whole game."

"And I thought you didn't know anything about baseball."

We stared at each other. His eyes were perfect dark brown, like coffee, and his lashes were dark. He was freaking unreal. He had even *tasted* good.

Delicious, in fact.

"Dad," Dylan broke in. "Ice cream?"

The moment broke. "Not tonight, kid," Ryan said. The corner of his mouth turned up. "Have a nice night, Kate. See you in the morning."

Week Three

"I DON'T KNOW," I said to my mother. "I think I might be bad at this."

We were sitting in a café after a few hours of shopping. I had weekends off, and this Saturday was spent with my mother, watching her buy things while I window-shopped. I was used to it; I had never had a job that made much money, a fact that made my parents despair.

"At what?" my mother asked, stirring her latte. "Nannying, or parenting?"

My mother was smart, well-informed, and beautiful. She was the kind of woman who could wear cigarette pants and a tossed-on scarf and look like a million dollars. She was wearing her hair in a short cut these days, which was chic and made her look ten years younger. The worst thing was, it was impossible to hate her. She was a woman of a certain income bracket and a certain age, but she wasn't a snob.

"Aren't they the same thing?" I asked her.

"Not at all," my mother said, amused. "We had a nanny for a few years when you were little. I tell you, I envied that woman for the fact that she got to go home every day."

"Thanks a lot," I said, pouring milk into my plain old coffee.

She smiled at me. "You were a good girl. Always so polite and well-behaved. But any little kid is a handful. As I'm sure you're discovering."

"Dylan isn't a toddler," I said, feeling oddly defensive of him. "And he's a nice kid."

"But?" My mother's brows rose.

"But it's weird being in someone's house every day," I said. Ryan's house, specifically. "I mean, their things are everywhere." Ryan's things. "And they're two guys, so it's a mess. I mean a *mess*. Dylan loses his backpack so often that I put a Post-It note on the front hall hook that says *Your Backpack Goes Here*. Then I put another one on the fridge that says *Clean the moldy stuff out of here*. And another one on the bathroom door that says *This is disgusting. Do something about it*." I ran a hand through my hair. "I'm being a bit bitchy, but really, *come on*."

Mom frowned at me over her latte. "I thought cleaning wasn't part of the job."

"It isn't!" I said. "It's just driving me crazy. Why do I care? I have no idea." I slumped in my chair and sipped my coffee.

"You don't have to do this, you know." Mom stirred her latte again, which meant she was about to lecture me. "You could take some time off while you apply for better jobs. That's what a trust fund is for."

Yes, I had a trust fund. It wasn't millions. In fact it was small, but it was enough for a while if I needed it. I'd had access to it since I was twenty-one, but I'd barely touched it. I wanted to make it on my own, doing whatever I hoped I would discover I loved. I had only dipped into the money when it looked like the rent wouldn't get paid or I'd go hungry. Which was luxury enough. The rest of the time, I paid my own way.

Most people didn't understand that, I knew. It wasn't something I shared with many people, because people get jealous and resentful when they know that you've inherited money you didn't earn. It was one of the reasons I wanted to figure out how to get by without it.

The problem was, I didn't know what I wanted to do. Since graduating college I'd worked meaningless jobs here and there: hotel clerk, florist, pet sitter. And my parents, who had footed the bill for college, were unhappy about it. I couldn't blame them, really. I was the definition of a bad investment, and as their only child I was the one they'd pinned their expectations on.

I just... couldn't. I couldn't pick a career and start a rise to the top. I wanted to explore, to wander. To find myself. The problem was, I'd been trying to find myself for four years now.

Don't worry about it, Amanda had told me once. *You're a late bloomer, that's all. Some people bloom early and some people bloom late.*

How late was I, though? Should I start to wonder?

"Mom, we've been through this," I said.

"I know, I know. But the pet sitting was bad enough. And now you're a nanny for"—her expression went sour—"someone called The Bad Boy of Baseball."

I gaped at her. "You looked him up?"

"Yes, I did. If you want to be a nanny, Kate, I'm sure there are respectable people I could find to refer you to. People who pay well. Couples, not single men. Did you know this man actually hit someone on the baseball field?"

I could feel the back of my neck tightening. And I could also feel, as I always did, the urge to do the exact opposite of what my parents wanted me to do. Something that would shock them and drive them crazy. I had spent my entire life behaving, being the only child, trying to please the two most important people in my life. I just wanted to be *unexpected* for once. A little like Ryan throwing that punch. That punch was nuts—right there in front of everyone, while the other man was mid-sentence. What must it feel like to *not care* like that?

I'd always cared, too much. And since I'd graduated college, I'd kept trying to care. But deep down, I'd stopped caring quite so much.

It was freeing.

I wanted to not care like Ryan Riggs did.

Suddenly I wasn't so upset by this conversation anymore. I shrugged. "Ryan isn't so bad," I said to my mother. "He's nice. And he's really hot." *And I banged him five years ago, which I'm still not going to tell you.*

Mom's eyes widened, and then she closed them, as if fighting for control. "Oh, Kate, you can't be serious. If only you had married Mark."

"I am not marrying Mark," I said.

"Well, certainly you're not, since he's married now with a baby and another on the way." This was a fact she brought up frequently. Mark had been my boyfriend five years ago, back when he was a fellow student, getting a Ph.D in economics. He was nice, he was smart, and I'd really tried, but I just *hadn't cared*. After I broke up with Mark, my parents had barely spoken to me for months. They only fully recovered after Mark got married and they could throw the "what could have been" in my face. Now it was all about Mark's babies: *See, you could have had a man who is not only stable and reliable, but potent.* As if making babies was an achievement on Mark's part.

Making babies was hardly a sign of a man's virtue. After all, Ryan Riggs could make them as easily as Mark could.

"You know," Mom said, "I'm still in touch with Mark's parents. I could ask if Mark and his wife need any help."

And that was it, really. That was what it came down to. The suggestion that Kate, the loser, could work as a nanny for her successful ex and his two babies.

"Mom, you have got to be kidding me."

"I was just—"

"The answer is no." I picked up my purse and pushed my chair back. "I'm not working for Mark. I'm fine where I am, actually. I've decided I like it."

"Kate."

"I'm not mad." Well, I wasn't *that* mad. "Just don't suggest that again, okay? I'll talk to you soon."

I walked away, heading back to my car. Maybe I wasn't on a great career track, but I realized that in a crazy way I was where I needed to be. I couldn't let my parents dictate my life. They'd come so close to making all of my decisions for me, including who I married, for God's sake.

Maybe I was a late bloomer, but it was time to be myself for a while.

SEVEN

Ryan

Week Five

RUNNING at six o'clock in the morning does something to my mind, my mood. I have a busy, shitty brain that never shuts up, especially about stupid shit: things I've done wrong, things I probably missed, things that could go wrong today or tomorrow, things I've never done wrong but probably could have, given the chance. Just because I think a lot doesn't mean I'm smart—I'm not. I just have a brain that never. Shuts. Up.

Running at dawn shuts it up. So does sex. But for the last five weeks there was only one woman who made me think about sex, and I still hadn't gotten her naked again. So I ran my ass off.

It was just me and the pavement, my feet pounding, my breath in my lungs. One of my first coaches used to shout three words at us every time we started a warmup: *Fire it up. Fire it up!* he'd bark while we groaned through situps, pushups, squats, those devil moves called burpees. *Fire it up!* Years later I could still hear his voice in my head every time I started a run, every time I felt my legs start to move and my lungs start to burst. When I felt that resistance in the back of my brain telling me to stop, I always shouted it down: *Fire it up!* And I ran.

My muscles took over, and my brain shut up.

I pounded through my nice suburban neighborhood, the one I could no longer afford. I ate up the ground around the corner and across the path to the local high school, which had a track behind it. At six thirty it was deserted and I could get my laps in until sweat soaked my back. My shoulder ached, and then it screamed, and still I ran. *Fuck you, shoulder. This is none of your business.*

It was a damp, cool summer morning, which was perfect. When it's cold, you keep running to keep warm. And right now I was so warm that sweat soaked through both of the shirts I wore. And still I kept going. I didn't want to stop.

Kate Washington was driving me fucking crazy.

She shouldn't. I knew that. Kate was nice and smart and good-hearted. She was responsible. She was good with Dylan. She worked for next to nothing, and—except for the constant rash of bossy Post-It notes all over my house—she didn't complain. Any idiot would know they had a good thing going, and no idiot would mess it up. I should leave her alone. I shouldn't touch her. Ever. At all.

I wanted to touch her everywhere.

I wanted her naked so I could lick every inch of her. I wanted to hear the sounds she made, because I had heard them before. I wanted to feel her body give the slow, hard little pulse it gave right before she came, because I'd felt it and I remembered every fucking second. I wanted to be inside her again, because when I was inside her five years ago it had been incredible. I got inside Kate and I forgot everything—baseball and money and whatever stupid things preoccupied my mind. None of it mattered and I was just *there,* completely *there,* feeling her and tasting her. There was no awkwardness, no weirdness, it was just hot and easy and we both came, her knees wide and my face against her neck, both of us sweating and happy.

I wanted that again.

I was hard up for sex. It had been three long years of me trying to be Good Guy Ryan Riggs, the former player who was suddenly a dad. At first I was exhausted all the fucking time—having a toddler is no joke, and the last thing you feel is horny. Then, when Dylan got older, he got smart. I knew full well that he'd notice if I was off spending my nights screwing women, or if women were coming over to screw me. He'd know if I was going on dates or seeing someone, because I was the main thing in his life and he was an observant kid. He was also terrified that I would get a girlfriend and desert him. So the trend continued: no sex for me.

But that wasn't the reason I wanted Kate. If I just wanted sex, I would feel horny for, say, the female fans who still came on to me, or any of the women who gave me the once-over in a given day. Opportunity wasn't the problem. The willingness of the female sex wasn't a problem. The problem was that, even when I considered it, I didn't want to lick any of those women. I only wanted to lick Kate.

She shouldn't want me to lick her. In fact, if she knew how badly I wanted to lick her, she should probably quit.

She had those big dark eyes. That red hair. The curls that sometimes lay against the line of her neck. The line of her mouth was fantastic—I had a lot of dirty fantasies about Kate's mouth.

Her lips. I had even more fantasies about the dip of her waist and the shadow of cleavage when she wore a V-neck T-shirt. I remembered those breasts: they were C cups, perfect in my hand, the nipples light rosy pink. I had fantasies about those too.

This wasn't new. I thought Kate was smoking hot when I first met her five years ago. I still thought she was hot. The problem was, I couldn't have her.

I slowed my run and stopped, putting my hands on my knees. My shoulder was screaming and sweat dripped from my forehead. Kate would be at my house by now, in my kitchen, helping Dylan make his breakfast before day camp. He preferred when she did it. I could stay out here and avoid her, like I'd been more or less doing for five weeks now, or I could go back and face her.

I straightened, heading back and taking deep breaths so I wouldn't look gasping and pathetic when I walked through the door. In the pocket of my running shorts, my phone beeped a notification.

I took it out and looked at it. *Meeting with the league rep, eleven o'clock.*

My shoulder throbbed, and I pulled the small vial of pills from my pocket. The league rep had left me four messages yesterday, and when I hadn't replied he'd simply scheduled a meeting and sent it to my phone, like he owned me. Which he did.

But not for much longer, most likely. I had no illusions as to what this meeting would be about: I couldn't play baseball, the only thing the league paid me to do. I had taken too long, been a liability too long. My shoulder had been fucked for too long, therapists or no therapists. Pills or no pills, I still couldn't pitch a single ball, let alone a nine-inning game.

The meeting would be to tell me I was off the roster. But they couldn't tell me I was off the roster if I didn't go.

I deleted the appointment and kept walking home, my

muscles iced up now. Fuck the league and their appointment. They could shove it.

The Riggs boys have always had a problem following rules.

They tell us it's part of our charm.

EIGHT

Kate

Week Seven

IT WAS SUMMER, and now instead of taking Dylan to school and back, we did other things. Day camp two days a week. His friends' houses. The park. And, today, baseball.

Dylan played the outfield—a term I'd had to Google—and he was good at it. Today's game was played in a field in Grosse Pointe Park. The grass was green, the breeze was hot, the sky was blue, and a bunch of seven-year-olds ran around the field. There were days this job really wasn't so bad.

I was sitting in the bleachers, wearing a navy blue flowered shirtdress and tennis shoes. My hair was tied up and I was wearing my glasses, because I was in a hurry to get out the door this morning and I hadn't had time to put my contacts in. Beside me on the seat were Dylan's backpack, a bag of snacks, his sweatshirt, my sweatshirt, a bottle of sunscreen, and a rain jacket. Seven weeks as a nanny had taught me to come prepared.

My phone buzzed with a text. I checked and saw it was Ryan. *Where are you?* he wrote.

I blinked. He was supposed to be at another doctor's appointment. *At Dylan's baseball game,* I wrote back.

I know. But where?

Oh, shit. I looked around. Was he here? *Tenth row by third base,* I wrote.

Okay, Ryan wrote back. *I'm getting to third base.*

I bit my lip so I wouldn't smile.

There weren't all that many people at the game today—just parents watching their kids, some of them sitting in knots. I was sitting by myself. Then the row of seats shook and Ryan dropped down next to me, slumping like he'd been sprinting. "I fucking made it," he declared.

He was wearing his usual jeans with a faded Tigers T-shirt. Today he had on a baseball cap, worn and pulled low on his forehead, the brim bent in that way of baseball caps that are well-loved. Dylan's favorite ball cap looked like a truck had run over it a dozen times, and there was no way he would part with it.

"He's going to be so happy you're here," I said. "He loves it when you come to his games."

Ryan looked at me. "You're wearing glasses."

Oh. I tried not to adjust them self-consciously. They were nice glasses, I thought. Fashionable ones with black frames. "I didn't have time to put my contacts in."

He was still staring. "I've never seen you in glasses before."

Now I could feel my face get warm. Was that good or bad? Why did I care? "Well, not everyone was born with perfect vision, the way you were," I said.

Ryan narrowed his eyes, and for a second his expression did that smoldering thing that made me weak in the knees. Then he relaxed again. "They look nice," he said. He looked past me at all the luggage on the seat next to me. "You have a lot of shit here."

"It's important shit," I said. "Dylan might get cold, or it might rain. He's always hungry after a game, so I bring snacks."

"I don't know how you remember all that."

"I know. That's why you hired me." I pointed. "They moved him to center field."

Ryan nodded. "That's because he's fast." He frowned and looked at me again. "Hey. You just said something about baseball."

"I know." I smiled smugly. "I'm learning."

We watched the game for a little while. It was oddly relaxed, sitting next to him, even though my skin was buzzing like someone had touched an electric current to it. A few of the women sitting close by did double takes, staring at Ryan. He didn't seem to notice. Double takes were Ryan's normal.

"You must be proud of him, playing baseball," I said. "He's taking after you."

Ryan was quiet for so long I wondered if he hadn't heard me, or if he had tuned me out. Finally he said, "Can I tell you something?"

"What?"

"I hate baseball."

I stared at him in shock. He was looking straight ahead, at the field. As I watched, he winced as if his shoulder pained him and adjusted the brim of his baseball cap.

"You hate baseball?" I said.

He nodded. "Always have. I didn't watch baseball growing up. I didn't have any baseball heroes. I only tried out for it when I was thirteen because a girl said she'd kiss me if I'd do it. I play it, but I've never liked it."

"If you didn't like it, why did you play?"

"Because I was good," he said without bragging. "Being good

at it meant I could get out of my house every day. Being good at it —at anything—meant I had a chance at something other than growing up to be the loser everyone expected me to be. Playing baseball was my only ticket out of Westlake."

I had never thought of that. I'd always assumed that Ryan lived and breathed his sport, like every other athlete seemed to do. "So your home life wasn't so good."

That got the hint of a smile, like I'd made a good joke. "I didn't have a home life. My mother left when I was two, and my father didn't give a shit about my brothers and me. We had a roof and occasionally some food, and that was it. Have you ever been to Westlake?"

I shook my head.

Ryan glanced at me, then looked back at the field. "Westlake has a literal set of railroad tracks in it," he said. "The Riggs boys were born on the wrong side of them. Everyone knew our father was trash, that we'd grow up to be the same. My brother Dex is only four months older than me because our father knocked up two different women. Dex's mother had Jace and Luke, and then she left. So did mine." He leaned back in his seat, stretching his long legs out in front of him. "When I started making money playing, I hired a detective to find my mother. She'd married some guy and was living in Florida. She was an addict with a record as long as your arm. She died of a fentanyl overdose two years ago."

I put a hand to my mouth. "Oh, my God. Ryan, I'm so sorry."

He turned to look at me. His dark brown eyes were unreadable. "It turns out she had a little bit of money, or her parents did. A trust fund that they'd locked her out of so she couldn't use it to shoot up. They'd declared her legally incompetent or something. When she died, the money came to me. It wasn't riches, but it's floated us for a little while. If I'm smart with it, I might be able to send Dylan to college. No Riggs has ever gone to college."

I looked out to the field and watched the small form of Dylan standing in the outfield, waiting for the batter to hit the ball. From here he looked almost comically small and vulnerable. "Can I ask you something?" I said to Ryan. "Where's his mother?"

"Thailand," he replied. "That's the last I heard, anyway." I turned and saw that his expression was blank and a little bit angry. "I knocked her up at a party when I was nineteen," he said bluntly. "We were both drunk. I actually had a condom on me and forgot to take it out and put it on. That's how drunk and stupid I was. The whole thing took about twenty minutes." He sighed. "She didn't tell me she was pregnant. By the time she had Dylan she was twenty, and she decided she was too young to be a mother. She left him with her parents and went on a backpacking trip to find herself."

Something sour turned in my stomach, thinking of that sweet boy out on the baseball field.

"Her parents kept Dylan until he was four," Ryan continued. "They started to have health problems, and a toddler was too much for them. So they showed up and dropped him off one day. *Surprise, you have a son, here you go, have a nice day.*" He shook his head. "That was a surreal day, I can tell you. And every day since has been just as weird."

"I can't imagine. Didn't you ever wonder..." I stopped myself. It was rude and none of my business. I bit the words back.

But Ryan guessed them. "Didn't I ever wonder if he was actually mine?" He frowned and crossed his arms, watching the field and thinking. "In those first few days, maybe. And then after a while it didn't matter. Everyone believed he was mine, and he had nowhere else to go. I definitely remember fucking Amber without a condom, so I did the crime."

Ugh, I thought. *Amber.*

"Besides, now that he's older I think he looks like me," Ryan said. "Don't you?"

"Yes," I said honestly. "He looks a lot like you."

"So who cares?" Ryan shrugged. "He's my kid."

I stared at him. "So this... Amber never came back from her backpacking trip?"

"No. Her parents say she ended up in Thailand with some guy."

Unbelievable. "Does Dylan know?"

"I had to tell him. What was I going to say, his mother was living in an enchanted fairyland or something? I told him his mother moved away to another country." He lifted his baseball cap, scratched beneath it, then put it on again. "He's had questions. He'll probably have more. I have no fucking idea how to answer them."

I'd never heard Dylan mention his mother. There were no photos of her anywhere—there was only one photo in the Riggs house, a printout of Ryan and Dylan in a selfie in a park somewhere, both of them smiling into the camera. It was stuck to the fridge with a piece of tape and I looked at it every day. That photo made me feel... something. I wasn't sure what it was yet.

On the field, Dylan had spotted his father in the stands. He raised his hand once, quickly, excited but trying to be cool about it in front of his teammates. Ryan gave him a cool wave back, the two of them a mirror image.

I reached next to me and picked up the baggie of animal crackers I'd brought with me. I crunched one and Ryan held out his hand. I gave him an elephant.

"Your turn," he said.

"My turn for what?"

"To tell me something." He popped the cracker into his mouth. "Tell me why you slept with me five years ago when that isn't something you usually do."

I felt my face go red, even though he wasn't looking at me. "How do you know? Maybe I do that all the time."

"Nope," he said, so confident that I wanted to punch him. "You don't. Though you told Dylan you go on dates."

"Maybe I do."

"Maybe you were lying."

I stuffed another animal cracker into my mouth. "Okay," I said. "The truth is he asked me once why I wasn't married. You know how innocent he is. And how do I explain modern dating life to this little kid? So I told him I go on dates, because that's what you do before you find someone to marry."

Ryan was amused now, probably picturing my awkwardness in this conversation. "Not bad. Go on."

"Well, then he wanted to know whether I would date *you*. And he seemed all worried about it."

"Dylan has a total fear that I'll get a girlfriend," Ryan said. "I think he thinks I'll abandon him if I do that."

"So that's why you don't have one," I said. Fishing. I was totally fishing. I had no shame.

He didn't seem to notice. "That, and the fact that I'm basically a fucked-up mess," he said easily. "But tell me the rest."

"So I told him no, I'm not dating you. I'm dating other guys. Lots and lots of other guys."

Ryan looked at me. "You said *lots and lots?*"

I dropped my gaze and looked for a giraffe in the baggie. "I may have gotten carried away."

"That explains it. He told me you have all these boyfriends. Tons of them. He wanted me to be really clear about that. I couldn't figure out why you'd say that to him when it wasn't true."

I dropped the baggie back in my lap. "It could be true!"

"Kate, Kate." He shook his head. "Give me a little credit here. I haven't had one in a long time, but I know women. I especially know women who sleep with a lot of men. They used to be my specialty. You weren't one five years ago, and you aren't one now."

It was that phrase that made my throat dry: *I haven't had one in a long time.* Because I'd been wondering. I wouldn't admit I'd been wondering—even to myself—but I had. I needed something to do with my nervous hands, so I unwrapped one of the juice boxes I'd brought for Dylan. At this rate, the kid would go hungry and thirsty.

I poked the straw into the box and said, "Okay, so I cut loose for once that night. I admit it."

"I know. So tell me why."

I sucked back some apple juice, thinking of how to word it. It was actually a relief to talk about that night, because I'd never told anyone in my life about it. I'd never been able to gossip about it like you always see women on TV do. It had always been a thing I didn't talk about.

There was literally only one other person on earth who knew it happened, and he was sitting next to me right now. Because he'd been the guy in bed with me.

"I'd been dating this guy," I explained. "We were in a relationship for about a year. My parents wanted me to marry him."

"And?"

"And for a long time I just assumed I would do it. I'd spent my whole life doing what my parents wanted. They had rules, and I followed them. That's what you do."

I glanced at him. He was frowning. After what he'd told me about his own life, I guessed that following rules wasn't a big part of his childhood.

"Anyway," I said, "I realized that I was going to marry someone—actually marry someone for the rest of my life— without thinking too much about it, because my parents said I should. I just woke up one day and thought: *What the hell am I doing? Who even does that?* And I didn't want to marry him. He was a nice enough guy, but I didn't want to marry him. He hadn't even asked—that was just something else everyone assumed. We would stay together, he would ask, we would get married, the end."

"What a load of shit," Ryan said.

"It was. It was!" I sipped the juice box again. "It was terrifying, but I broke up with him. Everyone was shocked. My parents wouldn't speak to me. And I realized that except for finishing college, I didn't want to do *anything* they wanted anymore. It was like I found my rebellious streak at age twenty instead of when I was a teenager like most people do."

"But you found it."

"It was so freeing," I said. "Like, incredible. Scary and fun at the same time. I could do anything. And then one night Amanda offered me a ticket to the benefit she couldn't go to, and I took it. And I met you."

He was quiet for a long minute. I wondered what he was thinking.

I hoped he remembered it as good. Because I did.

I remembered it as amazing.

The juice box crinkled as I finished it. "Your turn," I said. "Tell me why, in a room full of women who would gladly sleep with a baseball player, you picked me."

"That's easy," he said. "You were the hottest woman there."

I gaped at him—sitting there in my shirtdress, my glasses on, juice box in my hand. "No, I was not."

He rolled his eyes, like I was being ridiculous. "I have very high standards, Kate. You think I was settling?"

How he could be so hot and so punchable at the same time? It was an eternal mystery to me. "I think you're bullshitting," I said. "I bet you don't even remember what I was wearing that night."

He looked at me, and his gaze took in my face, my throat, and landed on my mouth, hot and dirty. "A black dress with a strap on one shoulder. The left one."

"Okay." That was right. My mouth was dry. I couldn't think of anything to say.

Then the crowd stood up and cheered, and an unintelligible voice came over the loudspeaker, shouting. The game was over. It was time to go home.

NINE

Ryan

Week Ten

MY WASHING MACHINE WAS BROKEN. I could fix it, but I'd had to order a part. So it was August, it was hot as fuck, and I was at a laundromat in the fine city of Detroit, sweating my balls off and trying to force quarters into a machine that had been installed when Bush Two was president. It was a Thursday at two o'clock in the afternoon, and it seemed like everyone in Detroit had no job and no washing machine, because every single one of them was right fucking here.

Kate had taken Dylan across the plaza to the variety store to get something cold. She'd told me when I hired her that she didn't do laundry, but she didn't know me very well. One of the things you learn when you grow up in the Riggs house is how to wash your own clothes, because no one is going to do it for you. Water and soap isn't that hard. Of course separating lights and darks is for losers, so you lump it all together and suffer the consequences. You also wear everything you own until it falls apart at the seams.

But Kate's bossy Post-It notes were sinking in. I had separated lights and darks today, which meant I had two machines. I had just gotten one going and was trying to get my quarters to work in the other one—the machine kept spitting them out—without knocking over the cup of soap I'd gotten from the vending machine. Ryan Riggs, world's number one father.

I was balancing a quarter in the slot when a voice said, "Mr. Riggs."

I turned. The quarter dropped and rolled across the floor. Three machines down, a guy picked it up and put it in his pocket. I wasn't about to fight him for it.

The man standing next to me wasn't here to do laundry. He was wearing a pressed dress shirt and brand-new jeans. His dark hair was neatly trimmed and he had wire-rimmed glasses. The top half was a corporate look, but the jeans shouted *league rep*. Guys who work with athletes—but aren't athletes—always dress the same way, like *I'm corporate but I'm also cool. I'm sporty, but I wouldn't be caught dead dressing like an athlete does.*

I recognized him. He was the league rep who'd been trying to get me to a meeting for weeks now. What the fuck was his name? Will, maybe.

"What are you doing here?" I said. I had sweat running down my neck into my worn-thin T-shirt. I was wearing jeans, but they weren't nice ones like his. I'd worn them when I tried to fix the washing machine, and you could tell.

"I've finally caught you," Will-or-whoever said. He looked me up and down briefly. The Bad Boy of Baseball wasn't looking so hot today. I felt a slow rip of pain start at my right shoulder and work its way down my back, like an earthquake creating a fissure. "You've been avoiding me for weeks."

"How did you know I was here?" I asked him.

"Well, someone said that you have a nanny working for you. And since we couldn't reach you, we thought perhaps she could help us find you."

I closed my eyes. Kate. They'd tracked down Kate. "My nanny is none of your business."

"Nevertheless," Maybe-Will said, "I finally have you in person. Since you won't come in to the league offices, we'll have to do this meeting here."

I grunted and turned back to my washing machine. Put another quarter in the slot and gently boosted it in. The machine ate it without spitting it out, so I fished in my pocket for another one.

"We haven't received any medical updates since May," Maybe-Will said. "You know that we're supposed to receive weekly reports."

"There's nothing to report." The pain had worked its way across my spine now and was digging into the flesh of my lower back. I had painful tingles starting on my right arm. I positioned the quarter very carefully, trying to mostly use my left hand. "Nothing's changed."

"Mr. Riggs, it's August," the rep pointed out. "We're mid-season here. We're aiming for a playoff spot, and if we get it we need to know if you're in."

The quarter went in and the machine lit up. I opened it and dumped my soap in before it could change its mind. We'd hit the playoffs the year before I got suspended. We hadn't won, but those had been some of the best games I'd ever pitched. "Listen," I said to him. "If I could pitch a ball, let me tell you, I'd be pitching a fucking ball and earning a paycheck instead of standing here doing this. Talking to you." I looked at him. "Get it?"

"I get it," Who-Cares-If-He's-Will said. His jaw went tight.

"So I guess I'll just have to give you these." He reached into the briefcase at his feet and handed me papers.

I looked at them. I didn't touch them. "What's this?"

I knew what it was. Of course I knew what it was. But I couldn't just make it easy for him.

"Mr. Riggs, you need to read this over and sign it. In light of the fact that you've been absent from the team and unable to fulfill your duties—"

"What's that?" a woman at the washing machine next to me said. She was black, wearing a bright orange halter top in the heat. She looked over my shoulder at the league rep and narrowed her eyes. "Is he a lawyer?" she asked me.

"No, I'm not a lawyer," Maybe-Will said.

The woman huffed. "I wouldn't sign anything in a laundromat," she said to me. "Not a damn thing."

"Is it alimony?" said another woman, craning her neck to see the papers. "If it's alimony he should sign it and pay."

"No alimony," I said. "I'm a baseball player and they're kicking me off the team."

"That isn't exactly true," the rep said. "There have been severe and repeated breaches of—"

"He sounds like a lawyer," the first woman said. "But he's kicking you off a team in a laundromat."

"I've been avoiding him," I told her. I could feel my shirt sticking to my skin and sweat on the back of my neck. Fuck, it was hot. "If I don't talk to him, he can't kick me off. He finally found me here. Unfortunately."

She huffed again. "Makes sense to me." She turned back to her washing machine.

The second woman was still watching me suspiciously. "You look like the kind of guy who'd have alimony," she said. "Alimony and child support."

I looked past her out the window to the parking lot. Across

the plaza, the door to the variety store opened and Kate and Dylan came out. Both were holding popsicles. Dylan was gesturing with his, telling Kate a story he was excited about.

Fuck. He was going to fire me in front of my kid.

"Just say it," I said to the rep. "Get it over with, for fuck's sake."

He blinked. "Mr. Riggs, the league is discharging you," he said. "You're off the roster. You need to sign these papers of resignation." He handed me a pen. "Frankly, you're lucky we kept you on this long, especially after you bloodied Bennett Harding's nose on the field."

The first woman turned from her washing machine, intrigued again. "You punched a brother in the face?"

"His name was Bennett Harding," I said, taking the pen. "I mean, come on."

"Yeah, I get it," she said, turning away again. "I'd punch that. I still wouldn't sign anything in a laundromat."

But I did. Kate and Dylan were almost at the door now, so I put the papers on top of my vibrating washing machine and signed them. The pain had its claws in my back now, and my arm was throbbing. My hand and wrist were almost numb. My body was mocking me; the idea of me pitching a game, getting any team to the playoffs and on to victory, was a joke.

I signed the papers and shoved them back at Maybe-Will, along with the pen. He took his time putting everything back in his briefcase. When he finally picked it up and turned around, Kate and Dylan were coming through the laundromat toward us.

Dylan was talking, but Kate's expression went very still. She had her hair twisted up off her neck in the heat, and she was wearing a sleeveless white V-neck shirt and dark green shorts that showed off her hips and legs. The curves of her calves alone would have brought me to my knees, but she was oblivious to it.

She held a pink popsicle in one hand and looked at me with wide eyes full of serious concern.

Will-Whatever took his shit and left, sweat darkening the back of his nice dress shirt. "Oh, no," Kate said to me in a low voice so Dylan couldn't hear her over the sound of the laundromat. "Is that the guy who called me? I shouldn't have said anything. He said it was important."

"It's fine," I said. The words came out tight, and I realized I sounded angry. Actually I was in pain. I took a deep breath and said more softly, "You didn't do anything wrong, Kate. He would have found me anyway."

She was still watching me, not buying my bullshit. "It's bad, right?" she said. "It's really bad."

"Dad?" Dylan said, picking up on the vibe. "Was that man mean to you?"

"Nothing I can't handle," I said to him. "Did you get me one?"

He held out a popsicle, which I could see was melting in its wrapper. "It's lime."

"Thanks, kid." I pulled up a cheap plastic chair and dropped into it, facing the washing machine. I tried not to groan as my back touched the plastic.

Dylan came and stood between my knees, watching the clothes slosh, his back to me. I opened my popsicle and put my arm lightly around his waist and watched with him. And wondered what the fuck I was going to do now.

TEN

Ryan

I SENT KATE HOME. I didn't need a nanny right now; I needed to give Dylan some dinner—luckily he loved tuna sandwiches—and think things through. Make a plan. Figure out my life now that, for the first time since I was thirteen, I officially was no longer a baseball player.

Fire it up, Riggs.

I took a long, hot shower, which did almost nothing for the pain in my back. I got out and put on some loose gray track pants, then went to Dylan's room to get him in his pajamas. He usually fought me on this—the more tired he got, the less he wanted anything to do with sleeping. I'd given up figuring out little kids long ago. I was only twenty-seven, and sleep was my favorite fucking thing in the world—when I could get it.

But I lucked out: Dylan was already in his pajamas. Even better, he was face-down on the bed, passed out, his stuffed cat tucked under his arm next to him. Kate had taken him to the pool today, and it obviously conked him out without the usual struggle. I turned out his light and closed his door.

I stepped out the back door onto the darkened back patio and pulled out my phone. I called my brother Luke in Westlake.

"Yeah," he said, because none of my brothers ever said hello to each other on the phone. It would kill us, honestly.

"I have a question," I said to him.

I heard the quick hiss of a beer cap being twisted off in the background. "Shoot," he said.

I pictured him in our childhood house, where he was living now with his girlfriend, Emily. We grew up in a big house on the wrong side of Westlake's tracks, a house that had been nice a hundred years ago but was now a run-down mess. Luke moved back in there when Dad went to prison for trying to run over his friend in a drunken argument. Yes, Dad was a role model.

Dad was still in prison, and he wasn't getting out soon. It turned out that the garage he ran—the one Luke took over when he went away—was a front for a stolen-car and drug-dealing business. Luke had shut it down, Dad was staying away for a long time, and now Luke ran the business clean with our brother Jace. Jace had moved in to the guest house behind the big house, but soon he was going to move in with his girlfriend, Tara. Westlake was turning into a regular home, and two of the Riggs boys were settling down.

I'd always hated Westlake. We all had. But now I pictured Luke sitting on his porch, drinking a beer, his hot girlfriend somewhere nearby, and I realized Westlake was the one place I knew best. The one place I didn't feel strange. I understood Westlake deep in my psyche, in my bones, and it understood me.

"Do you still need help at Riggs Auto?" I asked Luke.

"Fuck yes," he said. "Business is picking up and I had to clean out the staff. Again. One of them was informing to the crooked cop who was trying to frame Jace."

Tara's ex-boyfriend, a crooked cop, had tried to set up Jace for a coke deal. Since Jace just got out of doing a stretch for car theft, it would have put him away for a long time.

The pain in my back seized, and I winced for a second and tried to speak. "I'll come back to Westlake," I said as I patted my pocket, looking for the tube of pills, making sure they were there. "I'll work for you."

"Are you fucking serious?" Luke said. "If you're bullshitting me, I'm going to be very fucking mad."

Another wince of pain, this one slightly lesser. "I'm not bullshitting, Luke. You need cars fixed, I'll fix cars."

I knew how to do it. Cars were in the Riggs brothers' blood. We all knew how to fix cars. It was the only thing I knew besides baseball.

"What about baseball?" Luke asked.

"Baseball is done. I told you." I'd told him about my shoulder. In fact, I'd made a scouting trip to Westlake a few weeks ago to get the lay of the land in case my shoulder didn't heal.

"Well, that sucks for you, but it's good for me and Jace," Luke said. "We need good help, and all we get are shitheads. We can fix up rooms in the house for you and Dylan if you need somewhere to stay."

I winced again, and this time not from pain. The last thing I needed was to stay with Luke and his hot girlfriend as they banged night and day. It was just a reminder of all the sex I wasn't getting. "No, I'll find a place. I'm selling this house anyway. If you know anyone who's selling something good, hook me up."

"Actually I do," Luke said. "Mrs. Amano's house up the street is for sale."

I frowned. "Mrs. Amano was like ninety when we were growing up. She's still alive?"

"No, she kicked the bucket a few years ago." Mrs. Amano used to yell about getting her shotgun out whenever one of us went near her house, so neither of us had much sympathy. "There was some legal thing where the son and daughter fought for the place, but they've settled it and neither one of them wants it. They want to unload. It's on the market for a princely twenty thousand bucks."

Twenty thousand bucks. God bless Westlake's shitty real estate market. "Have you seen it?"

"No, I just have the story from Em. She knows all the gossip on the street now."

Of course she did. We'd gone to high school with Emily Parker and her fraternal twin sister, Lauren. Emily was blonde and popular. The fact that she ended up with my dark, broody brother was something I didn't contemplate too hard. "Get her to send me the real estate agent's info," I said.

"So you really are serious. This will be good for Riggs Auto, you know. Westlake's resident athlete celebrity coming back to town to fix cars."

Resident celebrity. It would have been funny if pain weren't lancing up into my right shoulder blade. "I see Westlake has as pathetic a celebrity landscape as ever," I said.

"This place's pathetic-ness is our gain. We're going to get business with you here. Mostly women. Just try not to bang all the customers, okay?"

"Jesus, Luke."

"I knew you in high school, dude. By the way, is the hot nanny coming with you?"

I'd made the mistake of telling Luke I'd hired a nanny, and it had taken him all of one minute to fish out the fact that she was hot. He'd never let me live it down.

Kate. Moving back to Westlake would mean I would fucking lose Kate. The pain lanced down my arm again, and I had to switch my phone to my left hand. "I doubt it," I managed. "Since she lives here."

"You've actually kept your hands off her. I can tell," Luke said. "You sound like you have blue balls. Way to have self-restraint, Riggs."

"Fuck you, Luke," I said, and hung up.

I dropped the cell phone on the table and hissed in a deep breath. A dog barked somewhere, and a car drove by in front of the house. Far off, I could hear the pulsing bass of some guy's music as he waited at a stoplight. The air was warm and dark. I could smell exhaust and gasoline and grass clippings. Summer in the city.

I waited for the pain to ease up. When it didn't, I felt in my track pants again for the little vial of white pills. This time I pulled them out and dry-swallowed two. I had just gotten them down when I heard footsteps coming around the side of the house.

Kate came around the corner. She was still wearing the white shirt and the dark green shorts, an outfit that shouldn't be sexy but totally fucking was. She stopped when she saw me.

"What are you doing here?" I said. I was saying that a lot today.

"Hey," she said. She bit her lip. "I, um."

I realized I was shirtless. In fact, except for the low-slung track pants, I was naked. She didn't know that, but something told me she could guess.

Fuck. I was making her tongue-tied. Why did that make me feel good for the first time today? "You've seen it before, Kate," I said.

"It isn't that," she said lamely.

"Yes it is. I realize it's been five years, but you got a pretty good look. In fact, I seem to remember you licking my—"

"Okay." She held her hands up, palms out, in surrender. "Okay. Ryan. I came back because I didn't feel right when I left earlier. I feel bad about talking to that guy. I had a bad feeling when I did it, and I'm sorry. I want you to know that will never happen again."

"He was the rep from the league," I said. "I've been deleting his messages for weeks. Until today, they pretty much owned me. They were going to track me down sooner or later."

"Maybe, but it shouldn't have been me that told them where you were." Her brows furrowed. "What a bunch of assholes, tracking down your nanny and putting her on the spot. Poking into your privacy. That's low. I have a mind to call them and tell them off."

I felt myself smiling at her. "You do that."

"It would get you in trouble."

"No it wouldn't because I'm off the roster. I'm fired. That's what that guy was tracking me down for."

Her face blanched. "To fire you?"

I held my arms out from my sides in a *here I am* gesture. "I am no longer the Bad Boy of Baseball."

"Oh, my God, Ryan." Kate put a palm to her forehead. "I am so sorry. Can they do that? Just dump you?"

"Considering I can't play baseball, yes, they can."

"What about treatment? Surgery? There must be something."

"I've looked at all of that," I said. "Have you ever heard of something called referral pain?"

She dropped her hand and shook her head.

"It's pain, but it isn't coming from the right spot. So you can have an injury in your neck, say, but you'll feel pain in your shoulder or the middle of your back. It could travel, which means you could feel pain in a different place every day. And they can't find what's wrong with you, because the problem isn't in the spot that's painful. It's somewhere else they can't find."

"And that's what you have?"

"That's the theory. My right shoulder is a problem, but they've done dozens of scans and there's nothing wrong with it. The pain moves around—my lower back, my upper back, my arms, the back of my neck. I've had days with shooting pains in my chest muscles and aches in my jaw. I've had massive headaches. No one knows what the problem is. All I know is, today I could barely put a quarter in the washing machine. I sure as hell can't pitch a ball."

She crossed her arms. The pose made her breasts look good beneath the white shirt—it pushed them together slightly, made them look plump and soft. How many pairs of tits had I seen in my life? I could barely remember any of them. I wanted to peel Kate's shirt off of her more than I had ever wanted anything. Certainly more than I wanted to play baseball.

"What about those?" she asked, nodding at my hand.

I looked down and realized I was still holding the vial of pills. "These?"

"I see you taking them," she said. "What are they?"

I held the vial up. It had no label. "Honestly, I have no fucking idea. I only know they work."

"The doctor didn't tell you what he was giving you?"

"These didn't come from a doctor," I said. "Not a real one, anyway. The guy who sells them to me likes to claim he's a doctor, but I have a feeling a real doctor doesn't sell illegal pills under the table to sports teams for three times their street value."

"Those are *illegal?*" Kate said.

"As illegal as hell." I looked at the pills in their little vial. "They aren't the only thing he sells. Uppers, downers, speed, steroids—if you need it to get through the game, he can get it for you. The fact that you risk failing the league's random piss tests is your problem." I looked at her shocked face. "Relax. I've never bought any of that other stuff. I mean, steroids shrink your dick, so you know from personal experience I'm telling the truth."

"Ryan, can you *please* be serious?"

"Kate," I said, "I am always serious about the size of my dick. Always."

"Jesus, Ryan. You've been taking pills, and you don't even know what they are."

She looked gorgeous in the shadowy light coming from my kitchen window, her face set in lines of concern for me. And those shorts—I could look at her legs all day. She was wearing sandals, her toes painted red. I wanted those feet on my shoulders while I made her come. And at the same time, I didn't deserve her —not now, not ever. Not for five fucking minutes.

"No, I don't know what these are," I said, indicating the pills. "All I know is that they take the pain away. For a little while, anyway."

"Stop taking them," she said.

"No." I'd have to get a new source now that I was off the team. Then again, Doctor Whozit probably didn't care if I was off the team, as long as I had money. "I like them."

"Ryan, your mother died of a fentanyl overdose."

That hit a fucking mark. I should have known that Kate was too smart not to hit where it hurt. Because aside from the fact that they took the pain away, I didn't want to give my pills up. I just didn't want to. Because they felt... good. When I took them, shit just didn't matter as much. Everything was fine.

So I took them a lot.

And I could keep taking them, and taking them. Even when the pain was gone.

Just like my mother, who had walked away from her two-year-old son for another hit.

Just like my mother, who had followed one hit with another until she finally took her last one.

I hadn't even known her, but she was inside me. She always would be.

"I'll be fine," I told Kate.

"Really? Are you going to promise Dylan that?"

The words were right there, ready to be spoken: *It's none of your fucking business. Back off.* It would be so easy to lash out, to hurt her feelings and make her leave. I could make it bad enough that she might never come back. I could say things that would make her never want to see me again.

But this was Kate, and I would rather carve my heart out with a rusty penknife than say any of that shit to her. So I said, "What does it matter to you what I do?"

She blinked at the question. "Because... because we're friends."

"Are we?" I asked her.

"Aren't we?" she asked back.

I didn't know. I didn't know what we were. All I knew was that I didn't want her to leave. No one had ever actually given a shit about me before, and I wanted her to keep doing it. I also wanted her underneath me in bed like she'd been five years ago, her back arched and her legs wrapped around me and her fingernails digging into me as she came.

I wanted her to like me. I wanted her to trust me. I wanted her to laugh at my jokes. I wanted her to think I was a good person.

I wasn't going to get any of those things.

"Can I ask you something?" she said.

I shrugged. "Whatever you want."

"You told me that you tried out for baseball when you were thirteen because a girl said she'd kiss you if you did it."

One stupid dare, and everything in my life went from that

point to this. What an idiot I was. I wondered what it felt like when you didn't regret every choice you'd ever fucking made. "Yeah. That's true."

"Did she?" Kate asked.

"What?"

"Did she kiss you when you tried out for the team?"

What was that girl's name, anyway? I didn't remember anymore. I remembered she had long black hair. She'd tasted like breath mints when I kissed her, probably because she'd gobbled a few of them before I did it. I remember thinking it was weird, kissing a girl who tasted like Mentos. "Yes. She did."

"Okay then." Kate took a step forward, putting her face further into the muted light. She uncrossed her arms. "I'll make you a deal."

"What deal?"

She held out her hand, palm up. "Give me the pills, and don't buy any more. Give them to me, and I'll kiss you."

I stood there, dumbfounded. I should have laughed or told her that was ridiculous. I should have called her naïve. Instead I just stood there with my blood pounding in my temples, unable to say a fucking thing.

Give them to me, and I'll kiss you.

Give up the only thing that took the pain away. The only thing that got me through the day anymore. Give it up for a kiss from a woman—something I could get any day, any time, from any woman.

Give it up for a kiss from *this* woman.

Yeah, I knew my answer.

I took a step closer.

Easiest decision I ever fucking made.

ELEVEN

Kate

I DIDN'T THINK he would do it. But he stepped forward and put the vial of pills in my hand without another word. Just like that.

It seemed like a big thing. Because I *knew* he didn't want to give up those pills. I knew he needed them, that without them he'd be in pain. When he put the pills in my hand, it felt like he was giving me a gift. Like he was trusting me.

"Make it good," he said, his voice low.

It didn't cross my mind that I shouldn't be doing this. I'd forgotten that he was my boss, that he was off-limits, that he was someone I shouldn't touch. In that moment I wasn't Straight-A Kate, and he wasn't the Bad Boy of Baseball. I'd forgotten that he was a chaotic mess and he'd only cause me trouble. Or maybe I hadn't forgotten—I just didn't care.

I dropped the vial in my pocket. Then I stepped close to him, put my arms around his neck, pulled him down, and kissed him.

And the fireworks went off.

He pressed his hands against my back and opened my mouth. I dug my fingers in his hair. I could feel his hard, gorgeous chest against me, his hot skin, his tight muscles. He tasted deep and heady, and he stroked his tongue into my mouth. I moaned and sucked on it. He walked me backward and I banged against the patio table. He groaned into my mouth and lifted me onto it like I weighed nothing. I wrapped my legs around his waist.

Ten weeks I had wanted this. Ten weeks. I wanted his hands on me every time I looked at them. I wanted his body against mine. I wanted his lithe, hard strength and his heat. I pulled my hands out of his soft hair and cradled his jaw as he kissed me, feeling the soft scruff of his nighttime stubble under my palms. His kiss had been practiced five years ago, pleasurable and wonderful. Now we were desperate, climbing each other like teenagers, our mouths locked, his teeth scraping my lip.

I could feel his hips between my thighs where I gripped him, the cloth of his track pants against my bare skin. So easy. I could just push them down—dear God. I made a soft moan in the back of my throat, pushing my hips against him.

He responded by running his hands up my back, bracing one on the back of my neck and the other on the back of my head. He broke the kiss and pressed his mouth against the side of my neck, going still. We stayed there for a long moment, locked together and panting, my arms around his neck and his powerful grip holding me tight. I could feel him breathe.

"We should stop," I said weakly.

He didn't respond for a long moment, just kept his arms around me. Then he lifted his lips from my skin.

"I'm going back to Westlake," he said, his voice rough. "I'm going to fix cars in my brothers' garage."

I felt the breath sigh out of me. My chest hurt. He was leaving—of course he was leaving. There was nothing for him here. I leaned my cheek against him, feeling his pulse. His skin smelled like he'd just come out of the shower.

"I'll get a house there," he said. "I'm going as soon as I can. It'll be a bigger house than this one. Plenty of rooms. Dylan will have to switch schools. It will upset him. He'll hate it at first. But I'll be closer to my brothers, his uncles. It will be good for him, and after a while he'll love it."

"What are you saying?" I said against his skin.

"I'm saying I'm not coming back," Ryan said. "And I'm asking you to come with me."

My breath stopped for a second. It was an insane idea, to follow him to Westlake. To live with him.

But it was an insane idea to leave him and Dylan, too.

What did I have here? My parents, who weren't happy with me and rarely talked to me. Amanda, who was busy with her own family. A room in an apartment with roommates who didn't care. A career that was just one random job after another, none of it meaning anything, none of it mattering. A life that was pieces, but none of those pieces fit together.

It wasn't much of a life at all.

Life with Ryan was messy and risky. Raising Dylan right—he was just one kid, but it mattered. It was important. It was crazy, but it could be wonderful. Or it could really, really hurt. More than anything in my life had ever hurt before.

But I had my arms around Ryan, my legs around him, my hands on his warm, bare skin. Maybe he wouldn't always be, but right now he was mine.

"That's a crazy idea," I said to him.

"I know," he replied. "But I can't think of anything else that makes sense. Can you?"

I was quiet.

He waited, and then he said, "Kate. Will you do it?"

I sighed.

"All right," I said. "I'm in."

TWELVE

Kate

Six weeks later

"A MUSTANG," Dylan said. "Or a Thunderbird. Or a Corvette."

He was naming his favorite cars—the kind he wanted when he grew up. We were on the topic because it was Saturday morning and we were driving to Riggs Auto to see his uncles.

"What color?" I asked him.

"Red. Silver!" He looked out the window, frowning seriously over this question. "No, black. Like Batman."

"Batman has a nice car," I allowed.

"Batman has *the best* car," Dylan said.

"Right, of course." I feigned confusion. "What's it called again? The Batcar, right?"

"The Batmobile!"

"No, no. It's the Batvan. Or maybe the BatSUV."

"Kate! It's the Batmobile!"

I was happy to see him happy. The move from Detroit to Westlake—changing houses, changing schools—had been hard on Dylan. There had been some bad days, some tantrums, some acting out. But now that he was here and settled in, he was turning into the old Dylan again, sweet and funny and full of energy. He was turning eight in a few weeks, and to me he already looked taller and older than when I'd first met him just a few months ago.

And Westlake was good for him. It was much smaller than Detroit and less dangerous. He got along with the kids at his new school. Ryan had been in Little League here and was still a legend, which made Dylan a rock star on his team. But most of all he liked being near his uncles, Luke and Jace.

I had never met Ryan's brothers before. Luke Riggs was the smoldering bad-boy type, dark and good-looking, the guy who would always have a cool car and drive authority figures crazy. Jace Riggs was big, scary, tattooed, and soulful. He was an ex-con who was quietly smart and liked to read.

They were both so different from Ryan, and yet they were obviously his brothers. They were rough, blunt, sometimes brutally funny. They hated just about anyone telling them what to do. They had grown up in the same hard childhood that Ryan had, and they had the scars to show for it. And like Ryan, they were pretty damn hot. I was allowed to think that, because both of them had girlfriends.

Luke's girlfriend, Emily, was a gorgeous blonde who was a cop's daughter. How that worked with a bad boy like Luke, I didn't ask. And Jace's girlfriend, Tara, was a lovely brunette who had started out as his post-prison counselor. They were both smart, competent women who didn't put up with any shit—as, I imagined, you would have to be if you were dating a Riggs brother.

Dylan loved all of them—his uncles, their girlfriends. I hadn't noticed how lonely Dylan was in Detroit until I saw him blossom in Westlake. He loved hanging out with his uncles at Riggs Auto, talking about cars all day. Emily and Tara watched movies with him, played video games with him, took him to Chuck E Cheese. I knew that Ryan and his brothers hadn't gotten along well for most of their lives—there was a fourth brother, Dex, who still lived in Detroit and was usually referred to as "batshit crazy"— but he had let that slide to let Dylan get to know his family. And it seemed to be working.

Ryan hadn't touched me since that night on the patio of the old house six weeks ago. He'd sold the house and bought one in Westlake, a few blocks from his childhood home on the wrong side of the tracks where Luke and Emily lived now. The house he bought had a full, private basement apartment with a separate entrance at the back—which became my apartment. I had dumped my old roommates and I lived there rent-free.

So Ryan and I were... roommates. I had my own bathroom and my own door, but every morning I walked upstairs into Ryan's kitchen and helped get Dylan ready for school. I ran errands, then I picked Dylan up again and we did his after-school stuff. And when Ryan got home I went back down to my little apartment, where I spent the evening alone.

It was, by far, the weirdest setup I'd ever lived in. I was part of the family, but I wasn't. I lived there, but Ryan wasn't my husband and Dylan wasn't my son. I liked my apartment—I had decorated it on the cheap and made it my own space—and I liked my independence, but there was no denying that in the evenings, when I could hear Ryan and Dylan upstairs watching a movie or laughing, I was lonely. I wanted to go upstairs and join them, eat popcorn and watch whatever they were watching, but that was too intimate. Too motherly. Too married.

And that kiss. Oh my God, that kiss.

Damn it, it was six weeks ago. I was mooning over him, or I soon would be. I was definitely heading into mooning territory. And mooning over Ryan Riggs was a bad idea. The only way I could think of to fix it was to find someone new and go on a date.

I'd think about that later.

I pulled into the parking lot of Riggs Auto and got out of the car, Dylan running ahead of me into the shop. It was ten o'clock on Saturday morning, the shop had just opened, and Luke and Jace had agreed to let Dylan hang out with them for a few hours today. He had brought his backpack so he could do homework or read in the shop's office if he got bored, but Dylan never got bored when his uncles were fixing cars.

Ryan worked for Riggs Auto too, but he and his brothers had decided that instead of working at the main shop, they'd open a new location. The new shop—also called Riggs Auto, because the Riggs brothers weren't big on names—was across town. It was, from what I understood, on the *right* side of the Westlake tracks. They'd put Ryan in charge of it, which sounded like a vote of confidence. Maybe after being the Bad Boy of Baseball, Ryan would square up, settle down, and do something respectable. Anything was possible, right?

Inside the shop, Jace was under the hood of a car and Luke was sitting near the front, on the phone. Tara was sitting on a bench near Jace, a coffee in her hand. There was a tray of coffees she'd obviously brought sitting at the front next to Luke, and I helped myself to one.

"Okay, here he is," I said to Jace and Tara as Jace straightened and looked around the car at me. He was taller than his brothers, hard as iron compared to Ryan's fluid grace, his hair and beard dark. I knew he'd done time for stealing cars, though he seemed very sweet for an ex-con to me.

"Thanks," he said as Dylan came running toward him, back-pack swinging. "We'll take good care of him."

"Just call me when you want me to come and get him," I said.

"What are you doing, Uncle Jace?" Dylan asked.

"I'll show you, man. Go put your backpack in the office."

Dylan took off.

"No, no," Luke said on the phone. "We don't do that here. You have to go to Riggs Auto on Emerson Street. Yes, that Emerson Street. You know where that is?" He paused. "Yeah, no, you definitely have to go to the other Riggs Auto for that." He hung up. "Why the fuck did we give them the same name?" he said. "Talk about fucking annoying. Hey, Kate."

"What do you have to go to the other Riggs Auto for?" I asked him.

Luke glanced at Dylan, who had come back into the room, and then at me. "Uh, nothing."

"Nice save, dude," Jace said.

The phone rang again and Luke picked it up, bowing out of the conversation.

I looked at Tara, who sipped her coffee. "Don't look at me," she said.

I wished Emily was here. Emily was emotional and you could read everything on her face. Tara, on the other hand, was an experienced counselor, so all she did all day was sit and listen to outrageous crap with a poker face. But Emily worked Saturdays in the hair salon she co-ran with her sister, so she wasn't here. She and Luke both worked six days a week.

I looked at Jace next. He was still watching me, guarded amusement in his gray eyes. He was wearing worn jeans and a plaid shirt. He shifted his wrench from one hand to the other.

"What do you have to get done at the other Riggs Auto?" I asked him.

"Nothing," Jace said, trying to look innocent.

As if to catch him out, next to me Luke said into the phone, "No, we don't do that here. You have to go to the other Riggs Auto. And it costs an extra twenty bucks, by the way. Cash."

Luke hung up, and Jace said, "Twenty bucks cash? Maybe we should try it, Luke."

"Hey," Tara said to him. "I'm sitting right here. The answer is no."

"Em would cut my balls off and hang them from her rear view mirror," Luke said, "so no."

I looked from one of them to the other. What the hell were they talking about? Ryan had told me that they opened a second location. That he was in charge of it. That he had a lot of customers so far.

It made sense, because apparently in Westlake Ryan was a sports celebrity. They all knew who the Bad Boy of Baseball was here. But even though he knew how to fix cars, he wasn't known throughout town as a mechanic. And the location was brand new, in a part of town that had competition. Yet Ryan had a lot of customers.

I pushed down the bad feeling in my gut. It wasn't my concern what Ryan did. He was my boss, and as long as he paid me it was none of my business. Dylan was my business.

Which reminded me, Luke had just said *balls* in front of a seven-year-old boy. However, the seven-year-old in question had his head under the hood next to his uncle Jace and didn't seem to be bothered by it.

"Okay, well," I said to the room, "I guess I'll go. Call me a few hours when you're ready for me to get Dylan."

I turned to leave, and Tara slid off her seat and followed me.

When we were outside, she closed the door behind her and sipped her coffee.

"Never mind the boys," she said. "They don't want to say it in front of Dylan. And they know you'll be mad."

"Say what in front of Dylan?" I held up my hand as Tara opened her mouth to answer. "No. You know what? Don't say it. Why does everyone think I'll be mad?"

She tilted her head a little, in that *I'm listening as your counselor* pose she did sometimes. "Well," she said, "you and Ryan. You know."

"No, I don't know. There's nothing to know." I pushed my hair back from my face in the cool fall wind. "I'm just the nanny, Tara. That's it."

"Um," she said, like a counselor again. "He brought you here with him and moved you in with him because you're just the nanny."

"That was to help Dylan adjust. And because..." It did sound kind of strange when you put it that way. "He trusts me. But there's nothing going on."

"That, I believe," Tara said.

I threw my hands in the air. "Okay, fine." Maybe I was overreacting, but I'd had *weeks* of unfulfilled sexual tension, plus a kiss I couldn't get out of my mind from the most gorgeous man on the planet. So I wasn't totally calm. "I give up on you. On all of you. I'm going to do some errands."

"Drop by Riggs Auto Two," Tara called after me, using the nickname the brothers had started calling it. "I think it's best if you see for yourself and decide your reaction."

"I'm not paying you for this session," I called back to her as I got in my car.

"It's free," she called back as I slammed the door. When I drove off, she was smiling.

I HAD THINGS TO DO. I needed groceries for myself, laundry detergent. I needed to pick up the pair of boots I had gotten repaired. I wanted to buy a new bra. I didn't do any of those things. I drove across town to Riggs Auto Two.

I had been here once before, when Ryan wanted Dylan to see the place before it opened. It was definitely in a nicer part of town than Riggs Auto One: there was a newish mall ten minutes down the street, and a row of chain stores around the corner. Westlake wasn't a particularly rich town, but it had its share of middle-class white-collar workers, and most of them seemed to live in this area. There was even an empty lot with a sign that said *Future site of Whole Foods*—a sure sign that the place was coming up in the world.

There were cars in the parking lot at Riggs Auto. Two of them had women standing next to them, chatting and seemingly waiting. They looked at me as I approached.

"What time are you?" one of them, a brunette with her hair cut in a fashionably short cut, asked.

"I'm sorry?" I said..

"I'm ten o'clock," the woman said. "Oil change."

"I'm ten thirty," the other woman said. "Broken headlight."

"If you're eleven o'clock, you'll have to wait," the first woman said. She jerked her thumb at the shop. "Nine forty-five is still finishing up."

"What a slut," the second woman said. She had long dark blond hair nearly to her waist and looked like she was in her late thirties. "She's had three tires changed this week. One by one."

I felt something cold in the pit of my stomach.

"My husband asked me what the twenty bucks was for," the first woman said. "I told him it was none of his business."

Both women laughed.

There was a hum, and one of the bay doors opened mechanically, revealing a car inside. It pulled out and drove off, the woman inside putting her sunglasses on and ignoring us.

"Here he comes," the ten thirty woman said. "This is the reason I showed up early."

There was a metallic sound, and the second bay door started to rise. This one wasn't mechanical. It was being pulled up by the person inside, revealing him bit by bit from the feet up.

Worn black boots. Beat-up jeans that fit like a second skin. Long, lean, muscled legs. A dark belt with a silver belt buckle.

Then his six pack. Those glorious abs, on full display. Bare.

The dark line of hair of his happy trail. Then his chest, the muscles of his pecs flexing as he pulled the door up. His nipples. His broad, perfect shoulders. His spectacular arms. And finally the flawless, clean-shaven, gorgeous, familiar face of Ryan Riggs.

He pulled the door all the way up, letting go of it above his head. The entire motion was a work of art, the kind of thing Michelangelo sculpted for decades to perfect. And there was Ryan, ready to fix cars. With no shirt on.

Suddenly I understood what the twenty bucks was for. Without the twenty, Ryan fixed your car with his shirt on. But with the twenty bucks, he fixed it bare.

He held his hands out from his sides in an I'm-here gesture.

"All right," he said to the women in the parking lot. "Who's next?"

THIRTEEN

Ryan

KATE WAS MAD. I knew it when I saw her face, there in the parking lot of Riggs Auto Two. Then again, I knew she'd be mad about this. It was the reason I hadn't told her about it.

I wasn't doing anything wrong, exactly. I was just fixing cars. But my customers were women, and they were here because I was me. And halfway through the first day I was open I knew I could make extra money if I offered to work with my shirt off. So I offered it.

And my customers paid.

There was no touching. Nothing dirty going on. I'd had a few offers, but I'd turned them down politely. I wasn't here to date or to fuck or to do anything other than fix cars. I was just doing it half naked, that was all.

It was an equal world, right? If women had to work at Hooters, wearing a low-cut top to serve wings, then I could do oil changes shirtless for a few extra bucks.

"I'm ten o'clock," one of the women in my parking lot said, raising her hand. She had short brown hair.

I pointed to the open bay next to me. "Drive in." I smiled at the other woman, who had long hair. "And you?"

"Ten thirty," she said, smiling at me. She pointed to Kate, who was looking thunderous right next to her. "I don't know what time she is."

"I don't think she has an appointment," I said. "I'll try and fit her in later." Then I reached up and pulled the door closed like a coward.

"See?" I heard the long-haired woman say to Kate. "It's like a *Magic Mike* show."

"Yes," came Kate's voice, quietly dripping with deadly venom. "I see."

Oh, she was mad. Really mad. I didn't see why, since we weren't together or anything. Even though she was living in my house, all day every day. Sleeping in her bedroom, which was beneath mine. Every fucking night.

It was driving me crazy. It was bad enough before, but now I pictured her naked when I heard the shower run downstairs, or I pictured her peeling her clothes off and getting ready for bed at night. (In my fantasies she always peeled her clothes off like a strip show, revealing a lacy bra and panties. My head porn was as detailed as ever.) I could picture her wearing nothing but a T-shirt, right behind a single closed door that separated her from me.

I was getting used to the feeling of wanting Kate—it was part of my everyday life. Wake up, fix cars, don't take pills or think about taking pills, want to lick Kate. That was my life. But I didn't make a move. She'd just moved in with me, and I was her boss. We had a history. She was smart and I was a fuckup ex-baseball player with no prospects. If we fucked, did that mean we were in a relationship? It might, since we lived in the same house. That was a bad idea, and it would give Dylan a nervous breakdown when he'd almost had one over the move already. So, no. I wasn't the smartest Riggs brother— that would be Jace—but even I knew this shit was complicated.

Being in Westlake was almost good. The pain in my shoulder had gone down some—I could usually kill it with Motrin. I didn't miss Detroit, and I definitely didn't miss baseball. Luke and Jace were actually half decent now that they were both back in town. My brother Dex was still an asshole, but I didn't have to see him because he was still in Detroit, doing whatever the fuck ex-cops did for a living. I didn't know, and I didn't ask.

I'd never held down a steady job before—baseball players don't have to. Don't get me wrong, we work hard training and practicing, but that isn't the same as clocking in and out every day. Answering the phone and taking credit cards. Jace worked the marketing and the books for Riggs Auto Two behind the scenes, but I was doing the rest of it myself—taking appointments, doing the work, taking payment with the computer system Jace had bought. It had only been two weeks, and I was exhausted. But Jace and Luke had given me a lecture about how Riggs Auto Two was an experiment, and if it was popular they would consider hiring me an assistant.

So I started taking my shirt off, and guess what? It was fucking popular.

And Kate was going to kill me.

We were open until four on Saturdays, and when I got home Kate and Dylan weren't there. *At the Ball Pit,* a note on the kitchen table said, written in Kate's loopy, girly handwriting. *I'll drop him at Luke's.* The Ball Pit was literally just that: one of those big ball pits that kids jump into and go batshit for. It cost six bucks and was a Westlake institution—not that my brothers and I had ever gone. The second part of the note, about dropping him at Luke's, meant Kate was avoiding me.

So I got Dylan from Luke's down the street, and we did our thing. Kate didn't come home until nearly ten, when I heard her door open and close. Dylan was asleep. I gave Kate ten minutes and then I went downstairs and knocked on the door that separated her from me.

"Kate," I said.

She didn't answer.

"Kate," I said again.

Finally, she growled: "Go away."

"You know I have a key somewhere," I said. "Maybe I'll go find it."

The door was flung open and Kate stood there. She was wearing leggings and a tank top long enough to pull down over her hips. Her hair was down in dark red curls around her shoulders. She was wearing her glasses. She was curvy and pissed off and hot as fuck.

"You're wearing a shirt," she said. "Congratulations."

It was supposed to be mean, but somehow it wasn't. Her voice was a little choked and had no bite to it. She sounded like someone who had been handed a mean sentence and told to say it.

I *was* wearing a shirt. An old gray one with a faded Redwings logo and a stretched-out neck. I'd thrown it on without thinking after my last customer of the day left, but now I wanted to rip it off again.

"Where were you tonight?" I asked her.

"Out," she said.

"Out where?"

"I was on a date."

Like hell. "With who?"

She looked at me for a second, her eyes dark-lashed and

gorgeous behind her glasses. Then she sighed and stepped away from the door, walking into her apartment. Letting me in.

I stepped in and closed the door behind me. Looked around. She had made it nice in here. It was a basement, sure, but the house was a backsplit and she had her own entrance with windows around it. She had a small sofa covered in pillows and blankets and a TV. There was a square dining table with a laptop and a stack of books on it. There was a bottle of wine on the kitchen counter and an empty glass, like I'd interrupted her pouring herself a drink. Next to the sink was a mug that had writing on it: *Give me coffee or give me death.*

I had never been in Kate's space before, her home. She'd spent months now in my space, but I'd never been in hers. Seen her things tossed around, smelled her smell everywhere. In fact, I'd never spent much time in any woman's space. For all the women I'd screwed, I hadn't looked around their apartments much. I'd never had a girlfriend. I'd gone from my all-male home to a bunch of bachelor pads to my house with Dylan, where we played video games and forgot to separate our whites.

"You've made it nice in here," I said.

She shrugged and walked toward her wine again.

She didn't offer me any, so I made a beeline for the dining room table, picking up one of the books and looking at it. "*Principles of Teaching*," I said, reading the title aloud. "This is a textbook."

"I know," Kate said, pouring herself a glass.

I looked at the receipt, which was sitting on the table. It was from an hour ago. "So you went on a date and bought textbooks?"

She leaned against the counter, holding her glass, and dropped her gaze to her feet. "Okay, so I didn't go on a date. I signed up for a course and I bought textbooks."

She actually seemed embarrassed about that. *Embarrassed.* "That is fucking awesome," I said.

She looked up at me quickly, like she thought maybe I was making fun of her. "Ryan, it's nerdy."

"Kate, I've never taken a course in my life. You want to be a teacher?"

She looked uncertain, and then her shoulders relaxed a little. "I think I want to be a tutor," she said. "I like helping Dylan with his homework, and a few times he had his friend Ben over for help too. I think... I think I could be good at it."

Shit. She could be good at it. She could be good at anything she set her mind to. "You would be great," I said.

"It won't interfere with my schedule with Dylan. The course, I mean. I'm taking the lectures and the exams online. I'll have to go in a few times, but..."

"We'll make it work," I said. "Why did you tell me you were on a date?"

She put her wine glass down on the counter, banging it a little hard. "I *could* have been on a date."

Something had her wound up tight, and I had a feeling it was the sight of me half-naked at work this morning. I held my hands out from my sides the way I had at the garage. It was the pose I always used when I was on the mound and a batter gave me shit: *I'm right here, come at me.* "Okay, go for it," I said.

"What do you mean?"

"Give me shit. You know you want to."

She ran a hand through the curls of her hair, exasperated. "Ryan, I do not want to give you shit," she said, and in the next breath she said, "Why are you *doing* that?"

"Doing what? Working shirtless?"

"And taking money for it!" she cried. She picked up her wine glass to hide how upset she was, then put it down again. "Those women were just *ogling* you. Didn't you mind?"

"I made a hundred extra bucks today," I said. "Cash. That adds up."

"You're not answering the question."

"Do I mind?" I had to think it over, because the answer was that deep down, in some buried part of me, I did mind. "Would I rather fix cars with my shirt on? Yes," I told her. "But not if it costs me a hundred bucks a day. I'm not a baseball player anymore. I need money."

"So you're willing to get naked for it."

"I wasn't naked. And women do it all the time." I shrugged. "My body is what I have. I've spent thousands of hours making it look this good. It makes me money. It always has."

"Then you should respect it," she said.

That hit a mark. Because my body and I had been on the outs lately. It had failed me pretty spectacularly, in fact. And the idea of respecting it—of respecting myself—what the fuck was that? No one had respected me since the day I was born. I didn't even know what that looked like.

"You think I let any of those women touch me?" I asked Kate.

She crossed her arms. "That's none of my business."

"Oh my God, you do," I said. "You think I'm in Riggs Auto Two, fucking women for money."

FOURTEEN

Kate

I STARED AT HIM. "I do not think that," I said. "I do *not*."

He was standing there, so fucking gorgeous, all golden muscle and chiseled jaw, his dark eyes ablaze with anger. I was so hot between my legs it was embarrassing—I'd been hot since he walked through the door. And I kept picturing him standing there at Riggs Auto, and the woman saying *It's like a Magic Mike show*. Like he belonged to anyone who had twenty bucks.

Like he didn't belong to me. Because he didn't belong to me.

I'd felt, five years ago, like he was mine. I'd felt that way when he'd kissed me six weeks ago. But that was stupid, because he wasn't. He made every woman feel that way—every woman he'd ever had, every woman who showed up at Riggs Auto. Dylan's mother. His crowds of female baseball fans. Everyone.

"Tell me the truth," Ryan said. "You actually think I'd do it, don't you?"

"No, I don't," I said. It was true. I didn't think that low of him —I just thought he should think higher of himself. "Now you tell me the truth. Have you had offers from any of those women?"

He actually rolled his eyes, as if this were inconsequential. "Jesus, Kate."

"You have, then."

"A few women have said they're open to it, yeah. The answer is no."

And that was it. The part that hurt so much. Because the answer was no now, but someday it might not be. Someday, maybe someday soon, Ryan would find someone. And she wouldn't be me.

"Shit," I said through clenched teeth, my jaw aching. "I really need to get a date."

"What does that mean?" he said as I brushed past him, heading for the dirty laundry basket in the corner.

"Nothing," I said, picking up the laundry basket and pushing open the door that led down the corridor to the laundry room. "Go back upstairs, Ryan. Go away."

But he followed me down the corridor, into the laundry room, which was dark. I was in such a hurry to get away from him that I didn't stop to turn on the light. I could see the washing machine from the light of the hallway, and I headed toward it, thumping my basket onto it.

"I'm not leaving," Ryan said. "What the fuck does that mean, you need to get a date?"

I dumped my clothes out, started sorting them in the dark. "It *means* that I told myself I'd go to a bar tonight and see if there are any single men in Westlake. Because I need to meet one. I pictured myself being all cool and collected about it, but I chickened out. I didn't go at all. Instead I went to the community college and signed up for a class. Because I'm lame and apparently I'm going to be single forever."

A big, strong hand came over mine, stopping me from sorting. And then Ryan's hard body was against my back, pinning me gently to the washing machine. He leaned down in the dark and scraped his teeth lightly along the sensitive skin of my neck.

My body went still. My breath. My heart in my chest. My blood. Everything stopped.

"Don't do that," Ryan said in my ear.

His other hand came down and now I was caged, my hips against the machine, his hips pressing into my ass, his chest—hot as coal through our clothes—flush against my back.

He leaned down again, and this time his lips pressed my skin before his teeth nipped me. "You lecturing me about respecting myself, Kate? Do not go to a fucking bar to pick up a stranger. Do. Not."

I inhaled a shaky breath, felt it go out of me in a sigh.

His hands left mine and moved to my stomach, his palms flat on me, and he slid them up, up. My nerve endings sparked to life all over my body. Because this was what I wanted—his hands on me, touching me, bold and demanding. I wanted that so badly.

Without apology he cupped my breasts through my bra and my shirt, his hands sliding over them like he owned them. He let their weight fall in his palms, traced his fingertips over my nipples. My brain whited out. I couldn't think. A moan escaped my throat.

"You think I put my hands on a bunch of strange women at my shop?" he growled. My entire body was sensitized now, and I could feel him pressing against my ass, his power and control as he gently held me where I was. "There is only one woman I want to put my hands on. Only one woman for months, and she's been driving me crazy since the day she came to my fucking door."

"Ryan," I gasped.

His hands squeezed my breasts again, his touch warm and firm. How did he know exactly what I wanted? How did he know? I was nothing but a knot of sensations, incapable of doing anything except want him.

"I shouldn't touch you," he said, and his hands moved down my body to the waist of my leggings. "We both know it. But I'm going to this once, because you want it so fucking badly, and so do I."

"Yes," I said. It had been five years since I'd felt Ryan's fingers on me. I was aching for him to do it.

He pushed a hand under my leggings, under my panties, and slid his fingers over me. We both groaned. He dropped his forehead to the side of my neck.

"Jesus, Kate," he said. "You're so fucking wet for me. You're soaked. Are you always this soaked when I'm around?"

Yes. It was an affliction, how hot I was for him. Here in the dark, with his hand so dirty between my legs, I could admit it. I was always turned on when he was near, and nothing made it stop. Not logic or morality or who I thought I was supposed to be.

He started to rub me, his fingers expert on my pussy, sliding inside me and out again. I clenched on him, my body's reflex, and when he felt it he pushed into me harder, sending a spike of pure pleasure up my body. I gasped and he put his free arm over my stomach, lightly bracing me as his incredible fingers rubbed me higher and higher.

"So fucking hot," he said against my neck. "I can smell you."

"Don't stop," I begged him. I moved my hips, trying to get more, more. I was trapped between the washing machine and his hard body, his arm holding me up, but I could rotate my hips just a little bit. I did it, and I heard him hiss in a breath.

"Say it," he said.

"Make me come," I said immediately, the words spilling out of me. "Please."

He slowed his fingers. This was different than the last time we were together. Five years ago had been beautiful, everything a woman could wish for in a night of pleasure with a gorgeous man. This was darker, needier, both of us chasing pleasure, stealing it in this dark room in secret. It felt dirtier and more free at the same time.

"Say it again," Ryan said, his fingers torturing me slowly. His voice was ragged.

"Make me come, Ryan," I begged him. "Please. *Please.*"

"You want it?"

"Yes. Yes."

"Say you want it."

"I want it," I whispered.

Finally, the pad of his finger slipped over my clit, right in the spot I needed. And again. And again.

The orgasm came over me in ripples, up and out, to the top of my head, down to my feet. For a long moment I could barely breathe. If he hadn't been holding me, if I hadn't been braced against the washing machine, I would have fallen.

I came down quickly, but I wasn't done. Far from it. He had barely pulled his hand out of my leggings when I spun around in his embrace, facing him. I pulled him down to me and kissed him, deep and hard. Then I reached down and unbuttoned his jeans.

He let me. He didn't say a word. I could see in the dark that his cheeks were flushed, and I could hear his harsh breathing. In silence I pushed open his jeans, pushed down his boxer briefs, and took out his cock.

Did I remember what it looked like? Yes. I remembered everything. The feel of his cock, its heat and weight in my hand. The smooth, hot skin. I curled my hand around it and stroked it, and Ryan made a strangled sound in his throat. I stroked it again and he let his head fall back, his eyes closed. It was the pose of a man taking absolute pleasure. And I was giving it to him.

We hadn't done this five years ago. He'd pleasured me, and then we'd fucked. In the one night we had together I hadn't had the chance to pleasure him, to watch as I made him feel what I felt. To watch him lose control. Now was my chance, and I was greedy for it. I wanted to see that more than anything.

There was come at the tip of his cock, and I used it to lubricate my hand as I stroked him. He sucked in a deep breath as I ran my tightened fingers down to the base, then back up to the tip again. "Like that," he said, his voice hoarse. "Jesus, Kate."

It had been a long time for him. He'd told me as much, and I had been working with him—practically living with him—for months now. The things I'd thought after our interview had turned out to be nothing. He didn't go on dates. There were no women coming out of his bedroom in the morning. He used to be a player, but the appearance of his son had made him change his priorities, at least for a while. I knew that the truth right now was that there were no women at all.

No women except me.

In this moment, I was the only woman. The one who was giving him intense pleasure. The one who was making him forget everything and let go. I was the only woman to see Ryan as he was right now, hot and hard and close to orgasm.

"Fucking hell," he said as I stroked him. It looked impossibly erotic, Ryan in the near-dark, his head thrown back, his jeans undone and his cock heavy in my hand. I could feel my own arousal as I stroked him, the throb between my legs where my underwear was already wet against my skin. All I had to do was pull my leggings and panties down and he could be inside me in seconds, bare and hard, taking me. I felt an ache deep in my belly —I wanted that. But right in this minute I wanted to watch him come.

He tilted his head back down and opened his eyes. Then, as I kept stroking, he reached under my tank top, up my back, and unhooked my bra. My breath caught painfully as I realized what he was doing. Still stroking him, I let my weight fall back against the washing machine as Ryan pushed my shirt up roughly from my waist, taking my unhooked bra with it and exposing my breasts.

He leaned in toward me and I felt his cock jerk in my hand. I stared down at us in fascination and put the tip against my belly, and we both watched him come, his cock jerking against my skin, the come spurting out over my belly and my breasts, streaking and dripping. It lasted a long moment, and then we both paused, panting as if we'd run a race.

He reached out a long, perfect arm and braced himself against the machine. We were both still staring at my breasts and my belly, coated in him. I'd never done anything like that before. It was the hottest sight I'd ever seen.

With his free hand Ryan reached behind me into the laundry piled on top of the machine. He grabbed a T-shirt and swabbed me off, getting every drop off my skin. He tossed the shirt behind me again and pulled my clothes down. Then, still caging me against the machine, he leaned in and kissed me.

I thought it would be a hard kiss, possessive and dirty. Instead it was hot and almost gentle, deep and strangely affectionate. He kissed me like he wanted to memorize me, like part of him thought he'd never see me again.

When he finished, my knees were weak, and it wasn't just from the sex. I wanted to live in that kiss. I wanted him to do it again.

I stared up at him, my body shaking, my lips sore. "What are we doing?" I asked him, my throat dry.

He looked just as shaken as I was. "It's complicated," he said, and then he turned and left me alone in the dark.

FIFTEEN

Ryan

THE LAST CUSTOMER of the day had left, and I locked the door behind her. I walked into the front office of Riggs Auto Two and picked up my T-shirt, pulling it on over my head. I was shrugging on my hoodie when my phone rang.

It was Luke. "What's up?" I said when I answered.

"Come to the house after work," Luke said. "Emily and I want to talk to everyone."

"What about?"

"Show up and find out."

I shrugged. "Fine, but I have to tell Kate I'll be late. Anything else?"

"Jace and I have run the numbers," Luke said. "Riggs Auto Two is making good money so far."

This should have made me feel good—I'd only been in business for three weeks—but instead I felt nothing. Probably because the reason I'd made money was because I had to strip my shirt off for most of the day. It wasn't because of my auto repair skills. I was good, just as good as my brothers, but I tended to get the easy work—busted taillights, flat tires, fluid top-ups. Mindless stuff, because everyone assumed I was good-looking and brainless.

What would happen if I just fixed cars with my shirt on? Would the business make as much money? Because after that hot, mind-blowing session in the laundry room with Kate five days ago, taking my shirt off for strange women bothered me more than it should have.

If your body is what you have, you should respect it.

"So the place is making money," I said to Luke as I pulled on a baseball cap. "So what?"

"We agreed that if the business is there, we'd hire you an assistant."

"Yeah?" This, I was interested in. It was tiring me out, working six days a week, doing everything. "You're going to find one?"

"We already hired him," Luke said.

"What the fuck—that was fast. Is he good?"

Luke's voice was weirdly cautious. "He's good. And he's available to start right away."

I heard the loud blatt of a motor on the street outside the shop —someone who needed a new muffler. "Luke, what are you talking about?"

"Listen, Ryan. He knows what he's doing and I think he's trustworthy. He swears he's going to do a good job. He probably means it."

Now there were alarm bells going off in my head. The blatt of the motor was closer now, pulling into the parking lot. I had a feeling of impending doom, hearing that motor. But no. Luke and Jace wouldn't do this to me. "He *probably means it*? Don't say it, Luke. Just don't."

"It'll be fine, I swear," Luke said.

"Oh, Jesus. What did you do?"

But he didn't have to tell me. I already knew. The loud motor in the parking lot cut out, and a car door slammed. A voice shouted, "Riggs!"

I hung up on Luke and dropped the phone on the desk. I walked to the door and opened it. "Oh, shit," I said.

It was my brother Dex.

THE RIGGS BROTHERS had never gotten along, but Dex and I hated each other. Neither of us could explain why. Maybe it was that, because of Dad's impregnating two different women, we were only four months apart. Maybe it was because we were competitive, and while Dex was stronger and meaner, I was better-looking and athletic. Maybe it was because Dex Riggs was a straight-up, all-out crazy asshole.

Everyone knew Dex was crazy. He always had been. He'd become a cop, which had surprised everyone, and then he'd flunked out somehow, which made more sense. No one really knew why Dex wasn't a cop anymore—whether he quit or was fired. Dex wasn't talking, and to be honest I didn't care. Detroit had barely been big enough for him and me to avoid each other, but we'd managed it for years. Now that I was back in Westlake, the best thing about Dex was that he was still in Detroit, miles away.

Except now he was in the parking lot of Riggs Auto Two, standing in front of a godawful wreck of a car—a ten-year-old Mustang, dark blue with a crazy-ass white racing stripe on the hood, two dented doors, and silver rims that were coated in mud. Dex himself didn't look much better than the car did: he wore a red-and-blue plaid shirt buttoned over a stretched white T-shirt, and his jeans had honest to God rips in them, not the fashionable kind. His motorcycle boots were older than the car. His dark hair was mussed, again not the fashionable way—in the not-washed-in-days way. He had a scruff of beard on his jaw and his eyes were bloodshot.

"You have got to be kidding me," I said.

"Greetings, little brother," Dex said like a vision from my worst nightmare. "I'm joining the rodeo."

"How?" I barked. "I thought you had a job in Detroit."

"Nope." Dex fired a single shot from a finger-gun at me. "No job and no apartment, as it turns out. I'm broke as shit. You've inspired me. I've come back to Westlake to stay."

"To fix cars? No fucking way."

Dex pointed at the sign above my head. "That's my name, too, and you're outvoted. So here I am."

A headache was crawling up the back of my skull. This was different pain than the shoulder pain; this was definitely more Dex-related. This was the last thing I fucking needed. I was going to kill Luke and Jace.

While I fumed, Dex leaned his ass against the Mustang and took a joint from his pocket. He lit it and watched me. His pose was casual and unperturbed, but anyone who underestimated Dex lived to regret it. His dark eyes were fixed on me and they didn't miss a thing.

"Do you even remember how to fix cars?" I asked him.

"Of course I do," he said like this was obvious. Which it probably was. "I hear you have a good racket going on here, brother, doing the work half naked for extra."

"No," I said. It was a snap decision, but I made it right then and there—no more shirtless work. I would never assume that Dex wouldn't fix cars with his shirt off. In fact, Dex would fix cars with his *pants* off, smiling at the women as he swung his dick. "I've stopped that. I don't do it anymore."

His eyebrows went up, but I held firm. I was kissing a hundred bucks a day goodbye, and I was very fucking happy about it. I didn't want to do the shirtless thing anymore. I was done.

"Okay," Dex said, "shirts on, then. Anything else?"

"Yes. Don't smoke weed while we're working. It will lose us customers."

He held out the joint. "Want some?"

"Jesus, no."

"Come on. You're not a big-time athlete anymore. No random drug tests. You can take anything you want."

He didn't know it, but that hit too close to the mark. I was off the pills, and I was staying off. I didn't drink, either—I got out of the habit when Dylan showed up and I never got in it again. "No thanks."

"Square as ever," Dex said, shaking his head and putting the joint between his lips again. "It's like you're not even one of us. Oh wait, you kind of aren't."

This was standard Dex shit—trying to get under my skin any way he could. He didn't care about our different mothers and never had, but he'd poke at that if it bothered me. It was why I hated him. I pointed to the sign behind me, just like he had. "That's my name too, dipshit," I said to him. "Show up at nine o'clock tomorrow, or vote or no vote, you're fucking fired."

SIXTEEN

Kate

EMILY PHONED me as I was hanging out with Dylan, eating Spaghetti-Os. "Hey," she said, "it's Emily. Remember me?"

Of course I remembered Emily. "Um, yes."

"Are you with Dylan? Can you bring him to the house?"

"I suppose so," I said, watching the kid clean his bowl like I hadn't fed him a snack an hour ago. "What's up?"

"Family meeting," she said. "You'll see."

"Emily, I'm..." It sounded stupid coming from my mouth. "I'm not family."

"Yes, you are," she said. "I want you there. And I want Dylan there. This affects him, too."

Of course. Dylan actually was family. This wasn't about me. "All right, we're coming," I told her.

Half an hour later we had walked the few blocks down the street to the original Riggs house. It was big and old, and it had been practically falling down until recently, when first Luke and then Jace had started working to fix it up. The front porch had new floorboards, replacing the old rotting ones, and the yard had been cleared of the bushes of weeds. Behind the house was a guest house, which had been empty since Jace moved out to live with Tara. There was a car in front of it now—a blue one with a white racing stripe and a bunch of dents. I'd never seen that car before.

Dylan ran ahead of me into the house, bounding up the steps. He'd been shy his first few times here, but it hadn't taken him long to treat the house like his own and get comfortable around his aunts and uncles. Now he opened the door and we saw a crowd of family: Luke, Emily, Jace, Tara, Ryan. There were also two people I didn't recognize: a woman with honey-blond hair and a man who was so obviously the fourth Riggs brother I didn't have to guess. I knew that the fourth brother's name was Dex, he was an ex-cop, and every time his name was mentioned Ryan looked like he'd swallowed a rotten egg. I gathered they didn't get along.

Dylan beelined to his dad, and I turned to find Emily taking my arm. "You're here!" she said, pulling me toward the woman I didn't know. "Lauren, this is Kate, Ryan's nanny. Kate, this is my sister, Lauren."

I'd heard about Lauren, though I'd never met her. She was Emily's fraternal twin sister, and though they certainly looked alike when they stood side by side, they didn't look like twins. Emily was blonde and vivacious, opinionated, while Lauren was darker, quieter, more reserved. She had a slimmer build than Emily, and she looked like she could fit in at a country club, even though she was wearing boots and a jersey dress.

She smiled at me, and then her gaze went to my hair. "Your color is great. Where do you get it done?"

"Lauren owns the hair salon," Emily explained. "I run it."

"I got it done in Detroit," I said, adjusting my glasses. My hair was naturally dark chestnut brown, but I liked having red added to it. I'd done it for years. "I haven't been able to do it since I moved."

"Come to the shop and we'll give you the family discount," Lauren said.

But I'm not family. The words wanted to come out of my mouth again, but this time I bit them back. If they wanted to give me a discount, I'd take it.

"Lauren." This was Dex, who had come over to us. He was good-looking—honestly, the Riggs genes were ridiculous—but he looked like the disreputable grifter who would get kicked out of Lauren's country club.

"Dex," Lauren said. Her tone was cool, but there was something underneath. Like she was almost happy to see him.

"You finally ditch Vic?"

"We're divorced now, yes," Lauren said.

"Excellent move," Dex said. "Let him bore someone else to tears." He looked at me. "Who are you?"

"This is Kate, Ryan's nanny. She takes care of Dylan," Emily said. To me, she added, "This is Dex."

"Hi," I said.

He didn't reply. Instead he looked at me, and something dark and mischievous sparked in his eyes. He grinned.

"Don't show fear, honey," Lauren said to me.

"Oh, man," Dex said. "This is *fantastic.*"

"What?" I said. "What did I do?"

But I didn't get a chance to answer, because Emily clapped her hands and walked over to Luke. "Attention, everyone!"

We all went quiet.

"Okay, I'll just say it," Emily said, hooking her arm around Luke's. "Luke and I are getting married."

We all applauded. I was pleasantly surprised, but Lauren and

Tara looked like they already knew. "Please," Lauren said under her breath when she caught my eye. "The first thing I saw was the ring."

I looked again. Emily had a ring on her ring finger, a slender band with a modest flash of diamond. It looked pretty.

"We're going to have a wedding," Emily said when the applause died down. "We're doing it right here in the backyard of the house. We got a justice of the peace and everything. Thanksgiving weekend."

"Suits and ties required," Luke said, looking at his brothers.

Emily turned to Lauren, Tara, and me. "Lauren, you're my maid of honor," she said, as if there was no chance Lauren would say no. "And I want you guys to be my bridesmaids."

My jaw dropped. Bridesmaid? I barely knew Emily and Luke. I had just moved to town. I was the hired help.

Luke turned to his brothers. "It was hard to choose," he said in his nice, deep voice. He looked happy and relaxed, less broody than usual. "But I choose Dylan to be the ring-bearer."

"Yes!" Dylan said.

"And my best man is Dex."

Even Dex looked surprised. I looked at Ryan and Jace, wondering if this had hurt their feelings. But Ryan was smirking, and Jace was looking into the distance, his expression carefully composed as if he was trying not to laugh. They didn't look offended at all.

"Oh, and no gifts," Emily said. "We want to do a thing, but we don't need a pile of stuff. Just show up and have fun. That's all we had to say. We have snacks. Announcement's over."

Everyone relaxed. Dex left, a disgusted look on his face. Emily took Dylan to the kitchen for yet another snack. Ryan and Jace came over to us.

"Well, that was weird," Tara said to Jace.

"It was awesome," Jace said, lightly touching his hand to Tara's back. He was grinning.

"I agree," Ryan said. "It was fucking awesome."

"I don't get it," I said. "Luke just picked your brother to be best man over you."

"Thank God. I don't want to be best man, and Luke knows it."

"Me neither," Jace said. "Dex doesn't want to do it either. But he's stuck with it."

I looked at Ryan. "You're getting satisfaction out of this."

"Out of watching Dex have to behave like an actual human for Luke's wedding? Yes, I am." Ryan grinned. "I'm just waiting for him to burst into flames, like sinners are supposed to do in church."

Lauren raised her hand. "Excuse me. You've forgotten something." She raised an eyebrow. "It's the best man's job to plan the bachelor party."

Jace and Ryan went quiet.

"I take it that's a problem," I said.

"Dex's parties are a little... infamous in Westlake," Lauren explained. "High school with the Riggs brothers was an adventure."

Tara looked at Jace. "I heard a story about a topless party."

"I was *not* at the topless party," Jace said. "Okay, only for a few minutes. Then I bailed."

"I was definitely at the topless party," Ryan admitted. He ran a hand through his hair. "Okay, yes. If Dex is throwing the bachelor party, we will have to do damage control. We don't need the cops to get called after all the heat we've been through. We'll try not to have strippers."

"*Try?*" I said. "Either you hire strippers or you don't."

Jace shook his head. "You don't know Dex. He doesn't have to hire them. The strippers come to him for free."

I stared at him. "Okay, well, come on. You guys aren't in high school anymore. You must have calmed down some by now, right?"

Next to me, Tara sighed. Lauren narrowed her eyes. "You know, Casey Simpson's junkyard was torched a few weeks ago. The last I heard, they never figured out who did it."

I looked from Ryan to Jace and back again. "You're kidding me."

"We had a good reason, I swear," Ryan said. "I just can't tell you what it was."

"It was a very good reason," Jace agreed. "But hell, this bachelor party is going to be a disaster."

SEVENTEEN

Ryan

TECHNICALLY, I had no reason to run anymore. I wasn't training for anything; I wasn't going to compete. I could sleep in every day and no one would know the difference. But my body didn't know how to do anything else. When I didn't run, I went crazy.

It was Friday night, Dylan was going to a sleepover at one of his new school friends', and after I dropped him off I was restless and at loose ends. Kate wasn't home. Maybe she'd gone to a bar to pick up a stranger after all, like she'd threatened to do. Maybe she was out doing something innocent. She didn't tell me, and I had no idea.

Which left me alone in the house with my thoughts, the throbbing pain in my shoulder, and a craving for the pills I shouldn't be taking.

I didn't have any pills, but I knew where to get them. I had the guy's number. I could call him, get in my car, meet him some-where, and be dry-swallowing a couple of pills within ninety minutes. Just thinking about it made me remember what it felt like to float, to not care, to feel the pain fade to a faint memory. To have that weird, groggy sleep where I was half dreaming. To think for a while that everything was fine, just fine.

The pain had eased off since I left Detroit. Since I left base-ball. Instead of agony it had become a throbbing ache, sometimes punctuated with stinging zaps, like a reminder: *Hey, asshole, don't forget that you're still screwed up.* Yet even without the pills the pain was much better than it had been in over a year, and I'd done nothing except dump baseball and come back to Westlake.

There had only been one doctor—I forgot which one now—who had gently suggested that what I was feeling might be at least partly psychological. "Stress and anxiety can play a large part in recovery from an injury," he'd said, tiptoeing around the idea that it was all in my head. "We don't fully understand the effects of stress on the body, but they can be significant."

"I don't need a shrink," I'd said at the time. "I need to play baseball."

Now I thought maybe I'd been an idiot. I'd spent most of the last year wound up tighter than a mousetrap, pissed at myself, pissed at the world, and ready to go off. The pain and the anxiety fed each other, both of them digging their claws into me harder and harder. I'd been frustrated and stuck.

Now that I was in Westlake and the league was behind me, the pain had started to give. But it was still there, because I was still frustrated.

I did an evening run, pounding through the neighborhood in the near-dark of fall. The leaves were changing fast now, and they rustled on the sidewalk beneath my feet. *Fire it up,* my coach said in my head, and in a few minutes I was in the zone, feeling my breath and my body move, my shoulder throbbing with each step.

I passed older couples going for evening walks and kids on their bikes.

I'd left Detroit, but a lot of the shit was still inside me, like garbage left on the floor when someone moves out. I was disappointed that I'd failed, even though I hated baseball. I was looking at a future of doing nothing but fixing cars, because it was the only skill I had. To learn another skill I'd have to go back to school, which based on my past record I would probably fail. I was worried about Dylan, because he was at his first sleepover and because I was always worried about Dylan. I was jealous of Luke and Emily. I still had this fucking pain, which made me want the pills. And I wanted Kate.

Here in the privacy of my head I could admit that I wanted her more than anything—more than I'd ever wanted another woman, more than I'd ever wanted to play baseball. Next to Dylan she was the only pure, perfect thing in my life, and I wanted every piece of her. I wanted to fuck her. I wanted to own her. I wanted her to own me. I relived the night I'd touched her over and over, the way she'd been so easy beneath my fingers, the way she'd given in.

That first night five years ago had been more than just great sex between strangers. It had been a chance, an opportunity, and I hadn't taken it. If I'd gotten Kate's number that night and called her again, my life would be in a different place right now. But I had been full of myself, so sure that more opportunities would fall into my lap. It was easy just to enjoy myself, then go home and go on with my life instead of trying for something. That was how I'd lived my life then—whatever was easiest, I did.

Two years later, when Dylan showed up on my doorstep, I learned: you can't dodge the hard stuff forever.

I was back at the house now, and I slowed to a walk as I approached the front door. I stopped and stretched, feeling my body protest. I wasn't even thirty yet, but at nineteen I would have been able to do that run almost without losing my breath. Then I'd shower, go party, and fuck someone new, so I could do it all over again the next day.

Where do you go, I thought, *when every choice you've ever made has sent you further to the bottom?*

I had no fucking idea.

Kate's car still wasn't in the driveway. It was still just me and the voices in my head.

I mopped my face and went into the house. Upstairs, I stripped naked and showered, letting the hot water soak all my aches and pains. I got out and dried off, wrapped a towel around my waist.

I walked out of the bathroom, into the bedroom, and Kate was there.

She was standing in the middle of the bedroom, in the light from the bedside lamp, wearing a silky negligee thing. It was navy blue, nothing overdone or trashy, but it was thin and short and sexy. I could see pretty clearly that she wasn't wearing anything under it. Her hair was down and she didn't have her glasses on. Her expression was nervous and hopeful at once. There was no mistake, absolutely none, about why she was here.

I went very still.

She shifted her weight and her gaze flicked down, over me. I watched as she got turned on, looking at me, as it pushed out some of the nervousness. But it didn't entirely go away, and I knew the reason why: She thought I might say no. She thought I might say *Kate, you should probably leave,* and usher her out the door.

And I could. I could choose one or the other.

What do you do when every choice you've made has pushed you further to the bottom?

I wasn't going to make the wrong choice this time. I took a step toward her.

She bit her lip, watching me. "Just tell me one thing," she said, stopping me in my tracks.

I stopped and waited.

Kate took a breath. "Tell me the first thing you said to me five years ago, at the bar at the benefit," she said.

I was shocked for a second. Not that she'd ask me that, but that she'd think I had forgotten. And she was right. If I'd forgotten, she should turn and walk out the door.

But I knew. Of course I knew.

"'I like your lip gloss,'" I said, quoting myself.

She smiled. There was relief in that smile, and happiness, and anticipation. And some nervousness, too. I recognized all of it.

She reached down and pulled the negligee up off over her head in one motion. She was naked underneath it.

I pulled off my towel, and I grabbed her.

EIGHTEEN

Kate

HERE'S the thing about having sex with Ryan Riggs: It's never what you think it's going to be. When you think you're going to get a one-night quickie from a stranger, you get a long night of orgasms instead. Then you get hot and dirty in the laundry room, his filthy words in your ear. Then, when you think he'd be cocky and have every reason to get you in bed again, he respectfully keeps his hands off you. And when you finally throw yourself at him, you get a different man yet again.

The fact was, I'd been thinking of different ways to throw myself at him ever since that laundry room encounter. I pictured myself surprising him by getting naked into his bed—the direct approach—or taking a more subtle route by asking him out for a drink or something. I could "bump into" him when he came out of the shower, maybe. All of these things required Ryan to be gullible, me to be outrageous, and Dylan to be gone. Preferably overnight.

I had so many crazy plans in my head that I came home from getting my color done at The Big Do, Lauren and Emily's salon— I got the discount, as promised—and realized that I'd forgotten that Dylan had a sleepover tonight. Dylan was gone for the night, and I'd actually *forgotten*. The shower upstairs was running, and my hair looked nice. Ryan and I were alone. I had a few minutes to come up with something. I had to improvise.

So I stripped, pulled out the only piece of lingerie I owned— it wasn't spectacular, but it was better for seduction than a T-shirt and sleep shorts—and I walked upstairs to his bedroom, waiting for him to get out of the shower. It wasn't elaborate. It was simple. I just hoped it worked.

It worked.

Ryan Riggs might be complicated, but in some ways he was very, very simple. I pulled off my lingerie and he jumped me.

He yanked off his towel—oh, praise God, he was spectacular —and grabbed me, tossing me onto the bed. Then he climbed on and kissed me, long and deep and hard. I dug my fingers into his hair. It got hot very fast, his damp skin against mine, his taste in my mouth. It wasn't a sweet kiss—it was slow and dirty, posses-sive, but at the same time he was reading me. He broke the kiss and nipped my neck as I ran my hands down his bare, taut back.

"Okay?" I asked him, because I could feel something fragile in him.

"Do not change your mind," he growled into my skin.

I wrapped my legs around him, felt his cock sliding against me, his hard weight on me, and a pulse of pleasure moved through me. "Don't change *your* mind," I said.

I like your lip gloss. He'd remembered. He hadn't even had to try; he had those silly words branded into his memory, just like I did. If he hadn't, I wouldn't have gone through with it. I couldn't.

But here we were. He was all smooth, sleek muscle, every part of him, his chest and his stomach, his hips and his legs. His back rippled under my palms. I ran my hands up to his shoulders, then down to his ass, which I'd wanted to grab for weeks now. It felt as good as I remembered.

He made a delicious noise in his throat, like I was driving him crazy, and then his hand was on my breast, cupping it expertly like he'd done the other night, my flesh spilling just right over his palm. He bent down and sucked the nipple into his mouth.

I arched my back as arousal cracked through me like a flash of lightning. "Jesus," I said.

"These," he said, cupping both breasts, then stroking the nipples with his thumbs, "are so fucking perfect."

My cheeks went hot. He'd been looking? "Well, I—" He sucked the other nipple into his mouth, and words left me, replaced by a pathetic mewling sound.

He stroked his hands down my ribcage, my waist, my belly, his big palms warm and sure. He followed his hands with kisses down my skin, making me shiver. "Grab the headboard," he said. "Hold on to it."

I glanced up. The headboard was metal with spindles. I reached up and pushed my wrists through the gap, holding on. The pose changed the shape of my body, pushed my breasts up and out, arched my back. I felt on display, which was obviously the idea. Even though I was just as naked as I'd been a few seconds ago, I felt like I was spread out for him. The thought made me hot and needy.

I looked down and saw his dark eyes on me. His hair was mussed. He had a five o'clock shadow, which made him look a little like the bad boy he was.

He ran his hands over me again, obviously liking the pose I was in. It felt like I was tied up, except I could let go whenever I wanted to. "Don't let go," he said, reading my mind. "I like this."

"I want to see you," I said.

He smiled. It was devastating, that smile. He braced himself over me on straight arms, looking down at me, so I could see his chest, his washboard stomach, the V of his hips that led down to his cock. "Like this?" he said, teasing.

I let my gaze crawl him shamelessly as I remembered to breathe. "Not bad," I managed.

"Not bad," he agreed. "Open your legs."

They were already open, but I pushed them wider. Now I was holding the headboard, my legs spread, completely on display for him—and he was braced above me, on display for me. We both watched as he lowered his hips and pressed his cock through my wet folds, rubbing me. I gasped and I watched his muscles bunch, his jaw twitch as he kept control.

He slid over my pussy again, and it was so good, but I wanted more. My hips pulsed up and he made a little sound of pleasure, moving with me.

"Fuck, yes," he said softly. "This is better than the fantasies."

I huffed a surprised and turned-on laugh. "You had fantasies?"

"Every fucking day," he said. "Didn't you?"

I couldn't answer, because he was rubbing my clit with the head of his cock, and I couldn't speak. He moved his hips in little circles, hitting it just right, and my head fell back, my eyes closed. "Oh, God," I said.

"Keep talking," Ryan said, still moving.

"Don't stop. Please."

"Very nice, Kate," he said. "I like to hear you say it."

He was commanding, in control, and at the same time I knew I had him. It was me he wanted—only me. I was turning him on. I was making him crazy. This big, hot, muscled man was all mine.

"Kiss me again," I told him.

He leaned down, and this time the kiss was slower, almost

sweet, his tongue gentle in my mouth. It contrasted with the very, very dirty way he rubbed his cock on me, the slick sound it made, the way I could feel it pulse hotly against my pussy, the way the head hit the nerve center of my clit, sending waves of pleasure through me.

Ryan broke the kiss. "Good?" he asked against my mouth.

I couldn't form sentences anymore, I wanted him inside me so bad. "Please," I said. "Please."

"Ask and you'll receive," he said, and then his weight was off me as he rolled to open the drawer of the nightstand. I was on the pill, but of course he wouldn't do it without a condom. He'd made that mistake once before.

He came back, ripping open a condom wrapper. "You have condoms in the nightstand?" I managed. "We just moved in."

"Kate, Kate," Ryan said, shaking his head as he pulled the condom out. "I'm nothing if not hopeful when it comes to you. Don't let go of that headboard."

I didn't. I held on hard as I watched him roll the condom on, watched him smooth it over his cock. *I'm nothing if not hopeful when it comes to you.* "I should have jumped you weeks ago," I said, just realizing it now.

"You should have jumped me the minute I opened the door that first day," Ryan said, as if this was obvious. "But we'll make up for it now." He hooked my knees over his elbows and pushed slowly inside me.

I let my head fall back, my eyes close. "Oh, *fuck*," I panted. This wasn't like last time. Last time there had been lots of kissing, lots of stroking to make sure I was ready. We'd done it under a sheet. Ryan had been almost gentlemanly, considering we'd started with his face between my legs, making me come.

He wasn't being gentlemanly now. There was no sheet. I was naked and spread for him, and he was on his knees between my legs, fucking me, and we were both losing our minds. I could feel myself clenching, squeezing him, and I could hear the sound of primal pleasure he made as he pushed all the way in. I was wet for him, but there was still intense pressure, which made the pleasure even keener.

"You're so tight," he said, his voice a strangled rasp. "Okay?"

"Yes." I was more than okay. "*Yes.*"

He unhooked an arm from my knee and used it to brace himself over me, keeping the other arm under my knee, keeping me open. "I'll go slower next time, but this will be a rough ride. That good with you?"

I opened my eyes and looked at him. "Definitely."

His pupils darkened, and he leaned down and kissed me. Then he started to move.

It *was* a rough ride. There's one thing about fucking an athlete: they're extremely fucking strong. And coordinated. He pounded into me and everything went white, my thoughts stopped, and all I wanted was more of *this, all the time.* My hands were slick where I held the spindles of the headboard, and I was glad I was holding on, because otherwise we might drive it into the wall.

And surprisingly, I could feel my orgasm building. He hit me just right with every thrust, and I could feel my hips moving, my muscles going slack and giving in. I panted his name.

"Come on my cock," he said, like he was reading my mind.

It took another minute, but I did. The orgasm came in slow, hard waves, and I dug my heels into the bed. I felt myself squeezing him, and Ryan slowed, stopped, buried his face in my neck as he came seconds after I did.

I lay there, dazed and orgasm-drunk, as I felt him get off the bed and go to the bathroom to get rid of the condom. There was a moment when I wondered if he'd be cold. *Well, Kate, that was great, have a nice night.* He'd been with a lot of women. He hadn't been cold with me five years ago, but he *had* left. He never asked for my number, and I didn't see him again.

I hadn't wanted to see him again. That night had been too raw for me. But that was then, and this was now.

He came back to the bed and turned off the lamp. Then he got in, flipped me easily onto my side, and curled himself around me, spooning me. His muscled arm curled around me, and his hand found my wrist, gently rubbing it.

I went soft against him. He was warm, and he smelled so good. Our bodies fit. We lay there in the darkness. I was sore and happy and drunk on him.

"We're doing that again?" I asked him.

His hand moved up my arm, rubbing. It was sweet, almost affectionate. "We're definitely doing that again," he said. "Rest up, woman."

I smiled in the dark. He rubbed my shoulder, touched his fingers along my collarbone. I wanted to tell him how good it felt. But I was already falling asleep, and then there was nothing but darkness.

NINETEEN

Ryan

DYLAN'S FAVORITE THING, when we were home, was to sit on my stomach while I watched TV on the sofa. He was at Riggs Auto Two with me now, and I was working under a car, and when I rolled out on my back he sat on me again, like he was sitting on a skateboard. The problem was he was nearly eight and he was pretty fucking heavy. But I didn't have the heart to tell him to get off.

It was after hours. Dex was gone, and I was doing some extra work to keep up, because even with my shirt on we had a steady stream of customers. Dylan was hanging out with me, because my kid loved hanging out in a body shop. It was in his blood.

Right now he was telling me about dinosaurs. A *lot* about dinosaurs.

"Which one is triceratops?" I asked, just to stop the flow of words coming out of him.

"Dad, I *told* you. Can we have cake?"

Honestly, this kid could eat like a garbage pit and still be the size of a toothpick. I didn't know where he got it. "Why would we have cake?" I asked him, my voice strangled because he was sitting on my diaphragm.

"Because it's Kate's birthday."

I stared at him. "What? It's Kate's birthday?"

"Yeah. I heard her talking to her mom on the phone. She said she didn't need to call on her birthday, because it was no big deal."

Panic shot through my veins. What should I do? Kate had said her birthday was no big deal. Still, was I an asshole if I didn't at least acknowledge it? We'd slept together. It had been fucking fantastic. Now it was her birthday. Yes, I was an asshole if I didn't acknowledge it.

"We have to do something," I said to Dylan. "Get her something."

"Why?"

Because I had an incredible night with her four nights ago. Because she's all I think about. Because she's saving my fucking life. "Because she's Kate," I said to Dylan. "She does a lot for us."

He thought this over. I knew my son: he needs a minute to think it through, but once he does it, he's in. "Okay," he said. "We can get her cake."

"Fine, but she needs a present too. What should it be?"

Panic again. I'd never bought a gift for a woman in my life. Perfume? Flowers? What the fuck? "What does she like?" I asked Dylan.

"I don't know." He scratched his fingers through his hair. "Um, books?"

I couldn't get her a book. I didn't know which one to get.

"She's pretty," Dylan said. "Makeup?"

We were both baffled. We had no idea how to buy makeup. "She's taking a course," I said. "A teaching course."

Dylan looked at me, and we both had the same thought at the same time. Like a light bulb going off over our heads.

"School supplies," he said.

BACK TO SCHOOL shopping was one of the highlights of Dylan's year. He had a lot of anxiety around school, but he liked to pick out pencils, pens, notebooks, those pink erasers. We spent an hour buying supplies for Kate, including a pencil case (Dylan insisted) and a protractor (Dylan insisted again.)

Then we got cake. There was no time to get it personalized, but we got a generic one that said *Happy Birthday* on it.

We got home, and I laid everything on the table. "Go get Kate from her apartment," I told Dylan. "Surprise her."

He was excited about it. He walked to the stairs on exaggerated tiptoe while I tried not to laugh. Then he crept down like a stalker.

I heard him knock on Kate's door. "Kate, come upstairs right now, it's exciting!"

Kate's door opened. "Dylan?"

"It's cake!" he said, totally blowing it. "It's your birthday!"

She came upstairs. She was wearing yoga pants, a T-shirt— her lounging-around-the-apartment outfit. She had her glasses on and her hair in a messy knot. I looked at her and my whole body went warm. After we slept the other night, we woke up and fucked again, and that time I did it long and slow, letting her almost come twice before she gave in and begged me to do it. Then I tipped her over the edge and listened to those amazing fucking sounds she made while I came inside her. One night with

Kate, and I was the most sexually satisfied man you've ever seen. I never wanted anything else.

"Oh," she said, looking at me, at the table. Her cheeks were a little pink. "Oh, my goodness. This is very nice."

"It's chocolate," Dylan said, still on the cake. Was I ever that innocent? I felt like I'd been born a ball of tension and anger. "Open the pencil case!"

So Kate did what she did—oohed and aahed over the presents, let Dylan show her everything and explain. She accepted a slice of birthday cake and ate it. "Tell me you gave him dinner," she said to me with narrowed eyes as she dug her fork in and Dylan attacked his.

I held up my hands. "He had dinner, I swear." We'd gone to the local Greek takeout place while we were out. "It was even good for him."

Dylan left to play his video game in his room, and I watched as Kate tidied the table and put the cake away in the fridge. "Don't do that," I said. "I'll do it."

"It's fine."

She wasn't looking at me. "What?" I asked. "What did I do?" I ran everything through my head, trying to figure out what I fucked up. I couldn't think of what it was.

"You didn't do anything," she said, rinsing the plates. She put them down in the sink and dried her hands. "It's just that..." She turned and leaned against the counter. "Birthdays were never a big thing in my house growing up. I guess I'm just not used to it."

"Birthdays were never a thing?" They weren't a thing for me either—if my father knew when my birthday was, I'd be shocked —but they were big for Dylan. We always went big for his birth-day. He loved it. "You were a kid."

"You've never met my parents." She smiled, but there wasn't a lot of happiness in it. "My parents are big on rules. Not in a mean way—they just like things to go their way. I'm an only child, and it was always sort of expected that I would do things the way they wanted. And they weren't big on birthdays." She frowned, staring at nothing. "When I say that out loud, it sounds pathetic. I'm twenty-seven today. Why the hell do I care what my parents think about birthdays?"

"Beats me," I said.

"You're right," she said as if I'd said something profound. "Fuck it. I *like* my birthday. Thank you for doing this."

I felt myself smiling. I was getting warm again. "You're welcome." I stepped forward, watched her cheeks go pink again as she looked at me. She looked soft beneath that T-shirt, and now that we were alone I was going to get my hands on her if she'd let me.

She didn't protest, so I took her glasses off and set them on the counter. Then I tilted her face up and kissed her. I started out nice, like a sweet birthday kiss, but she went soft and hot, her tongue licking me, so I deepened it.

Kate moaned softly and her hands twisted the hem of my shirt. I moved my hands down to her neck, brushing my fingers along it, then sliding down her back. She gripped my shoulders, and the next thing I knew we were making out like teenagers, her fingers gripping my hair, my hands on her ass.

Only when I heard the thump did I realize we had moved and I had her ass against the kitchen table. I lifted her on and pushed her back, still kissing her. Her feet hooked around the backs of my thighs as she wrapped her legs around me. There were more soft thumps as her birthday presents fell to the floor.

I broke the kiss and moved my mouth along her jaw, the soft spot in the corner beneath her ear, down her neck. I could feel her breath, the hard knock of her heartbeat. "We can't," she managed in a whisper. "He'll hear."

I knew that. I was far gone, but not so far gone I'd fuck a woman on my kitchen table with a seven-year-old upstairs. Still, I kept her pressed down, savoring how hot and soft she was. "I'm coming to your room after he goes to sleep tonight," I said in her ear, rubbing along the seam of her yoga pants, making her squirm. "I'm going crazy. I need to come inside you so bad."

She sighed, arching her back and closing her eyes. "You are so sexy," she said, her voice dreamy.

Something cool sliced through me. Because that was the only thing she could think of to say. It was a compliment; I'd heard it any number of times before. But coming from Kate, it felt different. *That's all this is to her,* the voice in my head said. *Just good sex. But that isn't all it is to you.*

And then, on the heels of that: *Of course. Why would she want anything else from you?*

I should say something. I should back out. But she was the only thing I fucking wanted.

It was far, far too late to save myself. And I knew it.

TWENTY

Kate

"OKAY, THE DRESS SHOPPING IS DONE," Emily said. "It's time to drink."

We were all at the Riggs house—Emily, Tara, Lauren, and me. It was Saturday, and we had just done an afternoon of dress shopping for the wedding. I'd been dreading it, along with the credit card bill, but it turned out much better than I thought it would. Luke and Emily had a budget as low as mine was: all of our dresses were bought at the Westlake Mall.

Emily had found a pretty jersey long-sleeved wrap dress in a dark cream color that offset her blonde hair. As for the bridesmaids, we found a dress in Ann Taylor that was a dark rich green, with long sleeves, a slightly raised waist, and a long, flowing skirt. The whole effect was pretty and perfect for fall, sort of *Lord of the Rings*-ish in color. The store had three of the bridesmaids' dresses and was willing to give us a discount if we bought all three, so we were in business.

The entire affair had only taken a few hours, but we flopped on the sofas and chairs in the Riggs house as if we'd been marching all day with the Marines. Emily only stayed on her feet long enough to grab two bottles of wine from the fridge, plus four glasses. Then she flopped along with the rest of us.

"We should have done a bigger party," Lauren said, leaning forward to open one of the bottles and pour. "You should have let me take us to a strip club like I wanted."

Emily pulled an expressive face of disgust. "Ugh, Lauren. Just no."

"Maybe some of us would have liked it," Lauren persisted in a big-sisterly way. Lauren actually was the big sister, I'd learned, by two minutes—and she never let Emily forget it.

"You've totally turned into a horndog since your divorce," Emily said. "It's creepy."

Lauren sipped her wine, unperturbed by the insult. "The boys are going to have strippers," she said. "You know they are. It's an equality thing."

This was the night: the bachelor party. We only knew that Dex was throwing it and that it was somewhere in Westlake. The rest was top secret. Ryan had managed to get Dylan another sleepover invitation, so Dylan was looked after until morning.

That left us women free to have a bachelorette. Except that Emily had put the brakes on doing anything except what we were doing: sitting around drinking wine. She'd appointed Lauren her maid of honor, then overruled her party ideas. This seemed like a pretty normal dynamic among the twin sisters, along with the arguing that went along with it. Tara and I just went along for the ride, trying not to take sides.

"Can we at least order a pizza?" Lauren said pointedly. "And then jump the pizza man if he's cute? I'd like to see another naked man sometime this century."

Emily laughed, pouring her own extra-big glass of wine. "Lauren, it isn't our problem that the only naked man you've ever seen in person is Vic."

"Don't remind me," Lauren said. She took a sip of wine and pointed to me and Tara. "That's confidential, by the way. That my ex-husband is the only man I've ever slept with."

"What is said at the bachelorette stays at the bachelorette," Tara said solemnly.

"That's true," I agreed. I poured my own wine and pulled my stockinged feet underneath me in the comfy chair I was in. Secretly, I agreed with Emily: I was glad we weren't going to a cheesy strip club. I liked naked men as much as the next woman, but something about strip clubs was crass and sort of uncomfortable.

Besides, I already had a naked man I got to look at every once in a while. A hot, gorgeous naked man.

It was three weeks since Ryan and I had spent that first night in his bed. We'd been together three times since then, each time with Ryan sneaking into my bedroom after Dylan was asleep. It was incredible. It was hot. It was secret. I had no idea what we were doing; neither did he. There was no plan, no blueprint for what was supposed to be happening. I only knew what *was* happening. It felt a little out of both of our control, and I liked it.

"I don't care if the guys have strippers," Emily said. "I trust Luke. I mean, he's all mine. I have him tied down. Absolutely." She lay back on the couch with her wine glass on her chest, her feet poking Lauren's lap. "Besides, it's possible I told Mom that the bachelor party is tonight. And she's a cop. And it's possible she has a few people on the lookout, just in case."

Tara looked up from her phone, which she was using to try and pick us some music. "You're having them *followed by cops?*"

"Oh, dear God," Lauren said. "Em, that is so low."

"I am not having them followed," Emily said. "What if they try to drink and drive or something? I don't trust Dex as far as I could throw him."

"Dex wouldn't let anything bad happen," Lauren said.

Emily stared at her. "Excuse me? Have we known Dex since we were fourteen or not?"

Lauren shrugged. "He's more protective of his brothers than you think he is."

"You seem to know him awfully well," Tara said drily.

"I hadn't seen him in ten years before this week, in fact," Lauren said. "I've just always given Dex more credit than the rest of Westlake has. But I don't want to talk about him." She turned her attention to me. "I want to talk about Ryan."

I hid behind my wine glass, taking a gulp. "There is nothing to say about Ryan."

Emily laughed. "Kate, I live with a Riggs brother just like you do. So does Tara. I guarantee you ovulate every time he walks in the room, whether you want to or not."

"Especially with a kid," Tara said. "Extra ovulation."

"My cycle is perfectly normal, thank you."

Lauren was looking at her phone, finding a pizza place to call. She gave me a quick, sharp-eyed look. "So is he good in bed, or what?"

I gulped my wine again and didn't say anything.

The room went quiet.

"Oh my God, Lauren," Emily said, staring at me. "Jackpot."

"I don't..." The wine had gone to my head, but suddenly I didn't care. I didn't have *anyone* to talk to about this. "Yes, he is."

"I knew it was happening," Tara said softly, almost kindly.

"It's nothing," I said. "We're just fooling around. In fact we, um, fooled around five years ago. So we're picking up where we left off."

Even Lauren looked impressed at that. "Wow. I've been ogling Ryan since I was a teenager, and I never got that far."

"Because you got married when you were ten," Emily said to her. She turned back to me. "Not that I've ever touched him either. Spill, Kate. What's going on? Are you two a thing?"

"No, no." The words leapt to my lips, automatic. We weren't a thing. If we were a thing, I would know it. "Dylan gets anxious at the idea of Ryan getting involved with anyone. He's already been through so much. It wouldn't be fair to him if it didn't work out. So we're just... friends with benefits, I guess."

"But you live with him." Tara had her sharp-eyed counselor look on, and I suddenly wished that this conversation had come up when all of us were much, much drunker. "That complicates things."

It's complicated, Ryan had said that night in the laundry room. Understatement of the year. "It's casual," I insisted.

"Are you dating anyone else?" Lauren asked. "Is he?" When I didn't answer, she said, "I'm sorry, honey, but that isn't casual. Not if you're living in the same house."

"Definitely," Emily agreed. "Get him to step up."

"I don't want a relationship right now," I said. "You all have jobs you love, careers. Emily and Lauren, you've built a business. Tara, you love what you do. I'm twenty-seven and I haven't found what I want to do yet. I just started my first teaching course. I need to figure myself out before I go in on a relationship—with anyone."

"That's fair," Lauren said. "But you can be his nanny, or you can date him. You can't do both."

"We're not dating."

"You don't *date* a Riggs boy, Lauren," Emily said. "I know from experience. You're all in or you're all out. She has a point."

"But the sex," Lauren said. "If they're not going to have a relationship, then she has to give up the sex. Think about that." She shook her head. "You're right. This is hard."

Now I was getting annoyed. Why did everyone know more about what I was doing than I did? "Look, it isn't hard. It's very simple," I said. "He's extremely hot. We're both single. We both like sex, so we have it together. It's convenient."

"For him, or for you?" Tara asked.

"Can we talk about something else?" I said, looking around the room. "Please?"

They took pity on me, and we talked about other things. Lauren ordered pizza. Tara plugged her phone into the speakers and put music on. It was fun; I liked all of them. I hadn't had a lot of girlfriends aside from Amanda, and they made me feel like I belonged. But I still had tension crawling up my shoulders from that word *convenient*. It seemed to linger in my brain like a bad smell. Along with the question: *For him, or for you?*

Jesus, why was this so damn hard?

"Listen," Lauren said, sitting next to me on the sofa while Tara and Emily were talking about something else. "About the career thing."

"I know," I said, draining my glass. "I'm late. My cousin calls me a late bloomer."

"That's just the thing," Lauren said. "I found what I wanted to do early, and I loved it for a while, but now I'm burned out. That's why Emily has taken over the day-to-day. It's the weirdest thing, because part of me still loves the salon and can't let it go. But the thought of going in there and working all the hours I used to makes me freeze up. I can't even *think* about it anymore."

I didn't know what to say. "I'm sorry."

She shook her head. "I'm not asking for sympathy. What I'm saying is that it doesn't matter that you haven't found your thing yet. Because those of us who found our thing early—even we don't do that one thing for the rest of our lives. I ran a business for years, but I'm still almost in the same place you are right now. Starting late just... doesn't matter. As long as you start."

That actually did make me feel better. I smiled at her. "Thanks."

Across the room, Emily stood up from her chair, her phone to her ear. "What?" she cried. "You're *where?*"

Tara grabbed her phone and paused the music.

"Oh, my fucking God." Emily put a hand to her forehead. "This is a disaster. Yes, it is, Luke. It totally is. I knew this would happen." She sighed. "Fine. I'll talk to you later." She hung up. "That's just great," she said. "Dex and Ryan got arrested."

TWENTY-ONE

Ryan

THE RIGGS BROTHERS had never had a bachelor party before. We should have known it would all go to shit.

The first problem was that Dex wouldn't tell us where we were going. The second problem was that we all had to go there—wherever it was—in one car so that I could be the designated driver. Dex's idea again. "You don't drink anyway, Babe Ruth," he said. "You're too fucking square."

"I *could* drink," I argued, "if I wasn't the driver." I mean, come on. Who wants to be sober at a bachelor party?

"Not tonight," Dex said, and that was final.

I knew he was trying to piss me off, but I didn't want to start an argument before we'd even left. I figured I'd do whatever I wanted when we got there, and if we needed to take cabs home, so be it.

"Why am I dreading this?" Jace said when he got into the

back seat behind me, so that Dex could navigate from the front passenger side.

"You're dreading it?" Luke said. "How the fuck do you think I feel?"

"Listen, shitheads," Dex said, slamming the passenger door of my SUV. "If you didn't want to come to my party, you shouldn't have made me best man."

"I've changed my mind," Jace said as I pulled away. "Making Dex best man was the worst idea ever."

"You always were the smart one," Dex said.

"It was still worth it for the look on his face," Luke said. I laughed, which made Dex glare at me.

"I notice you got your car fixed," he said.

The four of us had nearly totaled my SUV on a joy ride to the quarry back in the summer. It was a long story, but we had our reasons. "I fixed it myself," I said. "It took me three days and four hundred bucks in parts."

"Then my work is done," Dex said. "Turn left here."

We were heading away from downtown Westlake, so wherever we were going wasn't there. The car was quiet for a few minutes. I racked my brain trying to remember what might be in this direction, but it was still too vague. It could be anywhere.

None of us had spent much time together growing up, and we'd gone our separate ways as soon as high school was over. Dex had gone to cop training, I had gone to Detroit for baseball, and Luke had gotten in his car and simply hit the road, not coming back for eight years. Jace had stayed in town, working for Riggs Auto while Dad owned it—and since Dad ran a stolen car ring out of the shop, Jace eventually started stealing cars. Eventually he got caught and did twenty months in prison. He never admitted it, but I always secretly wondered if Jace had informed to the cops on Dad in return for a lighter sentence. It wouldn't surprise me. He hated Dad as much as the rest of us did.

But after all those different roads, we were all back in West-lake. Dex had moved into the guest house behind the Riggs house —it seemed he was actually finished with Detroit and truly broke. This was the first time since high school that the four of us had lived in the same town. And now we were even in the same car, not killing each other. It made me briefly wonder if maybe things would start to be different, if maybe we'd all find some way to get along.

I was about to find out what a stupid idea that was.

"Take this exit," Dex said.

"South Road?" Jace said from the back seat as I turned off onto an empty industrial strip that was depressing as hell. "What's—oh, no, Dex. No."

Dex patted his pockets, probably looking for a joint. "Surprise," he said.

"Ryan, turn around," Luke said. "No fucking way."

"What's on the South Road?" I asked. And then I saw it. A lit-up sign ahead. "What's that?" I slowed the SUV.

"Hey, hey," Dex protested. "Keep driving, Little League."

"Fuck you, Dex. What is that place?"

A guy honked his horn behind me—the only car for miles—and I sped up again. I pulled over in the gravel parking lot and we all stared at the sign. *The Landing Strip,* it said. *XXXX Girls.*

"You actually brought us to the Landing Strip," Luke said to Dex. "The worst strip club in Michigan."

I racked my brain. I wasn't a connoisseur of Westlake's shitty strip clubs. "Wasn't this place out by the old airstrip? I thought it got closed down."

"It moved," Jace said. "They reopened out here. And they added a massage parlor in the back."

I stared at Dex. "You're taking Luke to get a *hand job* for his bachelor party? Are you out of your fucking mind?"

"It's only thirty bucks," Dex said. "My budget is limited."

"I'm dead meat if I go in that place, asshole," Luke said. "I'm probably dead meat already. You want to ruin my marriage before it even starts?"

Dex found his joint and put it between his lips, though he didn't light it. "I called ahead. I know the bartender. They're setting aside a VIP room, and it isn't even the one next to the men's room. It's further down the hall."

"A VIP room at the Landing Strip with my brothers," Jace said. "Just thinking about it makes me want to be celibate for the rest of my life."

"I'm getting venereal disease just looking at that sign," I agreed.

"You losers could enjoy yourself for once," Dex argued.

Jace shook his head. "I think enjoyment is already out of the equation."

"Jesus." Dex opened his door. "Everyone out. We're going in, and Luke's getting a handy. That's final."

"Forget it," I said, staying put. "I'm turning around and we're going back."

Dex got out, but he left the door open and put his foot on the running board. "C'mon Riggs, where are your balls?" he said to me. "You're not even the one getting married."

The image of Kate flashed into my mind. Fuck, I did *not* want her to hear that I'd gone to a hand job parlor. "Fuck you, Dex."

"Oh, I get it." His dark eyes were fixed on me, laughing at me. "You've got it going on with that redhead nanny, right?"

"Shut it, Dex," Jace said from the back seat. "Back off."

But Dex's gaze didn't flicker. "Is she as hot as she looks, Riggs?" he said. "I don't blame you. She has a sweet, sweet ass. You been in there yet? I bet she'd like it if you bent her over and—"

I was out of the driver's seat, around the hood, and I slammed him hard against the SUV. "Do not fucking talk about her," I said. "Do not say another word."

"All right, all right," Dex said. "If you're not going there, then I'll give her a call. I wouldn't mind a shot at—"

I slammed him against the car again. Dex laughed, but I knew my brother. We'd had plenty of fistfights growing up. The one thing about Dex in a fight was that he always fought dirty.

So when he kneed me in the balls, I flinched away. He still grazed me, sending a shot of pain straight up into my stomach. And it was on.

He threw me to the gravel. I landed a kick to his kidneys, and he fell. He grabbed me, pushing my face into the gravel, and then we flipped and I did the same to him.

Behind us, I heard the doors slamming as Jace and Luke got out of the SUV. I paid no attention, because Dex had managed a punch to the side of my face, which broke my hold on him. He tried to get up, but I kicked him in the knee and he fell again.

"Jesus fucking Christ," Luke said, appearing behind Dex and yanking him away. I felt Jace's big hands on my arms, pulling me back. He was strong, even stronger than me.

I didn't care. I was seeing red. I wanted to punch Dex. I wanted to punch my fucking brother until he couldn't move for saying those things, for thinking them. I wanted to punch him for a lifetime of his attitude and his bullshit.

And what was worse, I wanted him to punch me. Because he was the only one who could, the only one who would. Dex was the only person in the world who would give me a proper fucking beating.

And like he was psychic, like he was reading my fucking thoughts, Dex laughed. "See, little brother?" he said to me. "You're just as angry as I am."

There was a flash of red and blue, the blip of a siren as a cop cruiser pulled into the lot. The doors opened and two cops from the Fell PD got out. I didn't recognize either of them.

"What's going on here?" the bigger one said.

Luke glared at them, still holding on to Dex. "You have got to be kidding. Where the hell did these guys come from?"

The second cop looked at the four of us—Luke holding Dex, Jace holding me—looked at the blood on me and Dex, then looked up at the Landing Strip sign. "You guys weren't planning on doing any soliciting tonight, were you?" he said.

And that was how I got arrested on the worst night of my life.

THEY TOOK us to the Fell PD station. They let Luke and Jace go almost immediately, but they kept Dex and me. They wanted to know if we were drunk, if we'd had anything to drink at all, if we were doing any drugs. They wanted to know why we were at the Landing Strip. They wanted to know why we were fighting. They kept asking questions and disappearing again, leaving us alone in a windowless interrogation room.

"They're trying to find something," Dex said after the third round of questions.

We were sitting in two folding chairs, side by side, staring at a wall. They hadn't said we could go yet. "What do you mean, they're trying to find something?" I asked.

Dex glanced at me. He had specks of blood all over the side of his face from the gravel, just like I did. I also had a bruise near my temple where he'd clocked me—I could feel it throbbing—and my stomach was still turning from the knee in the balls. Technically Dex had won that fight, just like he won every other fight.

"We're Riggs boys," he said. "Mike Riggs' sons. We were fighting in the parking lot of a skeevy strip joint with an illegal massage parlor in the back. They're so close to locking us up like they want to, but they can't quite figure out how. So they make us sit here while they talk about it."

I stared at him. He was probably right, since he'd spent years as a cop. "They want us that bad?"

"Sure," Dex said. He didn't even seem mad anymore, at me or at anyone. "They're drooling to put the rest of us in prison with Dad. They've sweated Luke twice. They've raided Riggs Auto looking for drugs. They've set Jace up, trying to put him away." He shook his head. "Right now they're on the other side of that door, trying to figure out their play. They're pissed that they could only keep you and me, not the others."

I couldn't get my head around it. "How did they know where we were?"

"Seriously, Riggs, get a brain," Dex said. "Emily's mother is one of Fell PD's most prominent cops. For sure she knew that tonight was the night of the bachelor party."

"So they were keeping an eye on us? Are you kidding me?"

Dex shrugged.

"And you figured that, and you still brought us to the Landing Strip," I said. "Why?"

"Because," Dex said, "there is nothing I like more in life than driving cops nuts. Especially Fell cops. Did you see the looks on their faces when they left just now? They looked like someone farted. I live for that shit."

"Dex, I have a kid," I said. "I know you like to stir the shit, but if I get arrested, I'm fucked."

He rolled his eyes. "Relax, Babe Ruth. You were never in trouble. You're the good one, remember? The Little League champion."

"Minor league, not little league. *Minor* league."

"Whatever. If it came down to it, I would have just said I attacked you first. They'd believe me. The Fell PD would love nothing more than to book me for assault."

"You are a very, very fucked-up man. Do you know that?"

"I'm aware," Dex said.

My brain ticked over. "That shit you said about Kate. You didn't even mean that, did you? You're not even interested in her. So why did you say that shit? Just to make me mad?"

"Listen," Dex said. He scrubbed a hand through his messy hair. "How long has she worked for you?"

I thought back. "Since June."

"So, like three months? Longer? And you don't want her? Come on, Ryan. Are you fucking dense?"

I thought of the last three weeks, of how Kate and I were together. I didn't know what to do about it. "It's complicated," I said.

"Not that complicated," Dex said. "Wake the fuck up. You have two people who give a shit about you. You always were the lucky one. You know how many people give a shit about me? Zero. Think about that for a second. Then think about whether you want to be an idiot about your redheaded nanny, or whether you want to be smart for once."

The door opened and one of the cops walked in. He looked defeated. "Okay, you two can go. One of our guys will take you back to your car."

"Never mind," Dex said, getting out of his chair. "I know my way home. Later, assholes." He walked out the door and was gone.

TWENTY-TWO

Kate

I LAY in bed in my little apartment, staring at the ceiling as I heard Ryan come through the door upstairs. It was two o'clock in the morning. The girls had all had too much wine at our bachelorette party to drive, so none of us had been able to pick any of the Riggs boys up from the police station. The party broke up with a whimper instead of a bang as we all went home.

I wondered if I should go upstairs and talk to him, ask him if he was okay. But if I did, he'd know that I was lying awake, waiting for him and worrying. And I didn't know if that was something we were doing—waiting and worrying about each other in the middle of the night. What if he was tired and he brushed me off? Or what if I went upstairs and he offered sex? Should I say no to him? Would I even be able to?

Is it convenient for him, or for you?

Did I even want convenient? I didn't know anymore.

I pulled the covers over me and rolled over. I wouldn't go upstairs. I'd go to sleep. He probably wanted to go to sleep, anyway.

I heard his footsteps move softly above my head. He was trying to be quiet, considerate. The steps came to the basement door and stopped there for a long minute.

I held my breath.

Then the footsteps moved away and disappeared upstairs. I closed my eyes in the dark and tried to sleep.

SATURDAY WAS MY DAY OFF. I had a Saturday class at the college and a lecture in the afternoon—my course was structured on weekends, for working people. I was in the kitchen at eight in the morning, groggily drinking a glass of juice, when Ryan came downstairs, freshly showered, wearing jeans and a dark gray Henley.

"Your face!" I said when I saw him.

"Yeah." He gently touched the left side of his face, which was peppered with little red scuffs. He hadn't shaved this morning, probably because it stung too much. He had a shadow of dark scruff on his jaw that looked almost unbearably sexy. "Dex and I got into it last night."

I put down my glass. "You got into it? What does that mean?"

He sighed and opened the fridge. "We may have rubbed each other's faces in a gravel parking lot."

I stepped closer, checking out the purpling bruise on his temple. "And he punched you."

"And he kneed me in the balls." He pulled the orange juice container from the fridge. I bit my lip, and he smiled at me. "Don't worry, Kate. They'll recover."

And there it was—that crazy, crazy arc of sexual energy that always showed up between us. I wanted to touch him. My palms practically itched with the urge. But it was eight o'clock in the morning, and I had to get to class while Ryan had to go pick up his son.

"Okay," I said after we smoldered at each other for a long minute. "Um. Did you end up with a criminal record?"

"Nope." Ryan took a glass from the cupboard. "They sweated us a bit and let us go. Turns out it isn't illegal to have a fistfight with your brother in the parking lot of a hand job parlor."

"A *hand job parlor?*"

Ryan winced. "We didn't go in. Dex wanted to and the rest of us didn't. That's how the fight started."

Oh, my God. If Luke even breathed the air in a hand job parlor, Emily would kill him. And if Ryan went in there, I'd kill him, too.

Except that Emily and Luke were getting married, and Ryan and I were casual.

Right.

"So you don't make a habit of paying for hand jobs?" I couldn't resist saying.

"Jesus, no," Ryan said. "I get that I've been living like a monk since Dylan showed up, but my own hand works just fine. I haven't stooped quite that low."

I felt myself blushing. It made no sense—we'd been naked together a number of times now. I shouldn't get all hot and bothered at the idea of him masturbating. "So I guess you hate Dex more than ever," I said to change the subject.

Ryan took a long drink of juice, then put his glass down, his expression thoughtful. "No, I don't," he said finally. "Turns out I don't hate him at all."

I felt my eyebrows rise. "Really? That's new."

He scratched his chin. "Did you ever hear about the time I punched a guy in the middle of the game?"

"Yeah," I said, picking up my own glass and leaning against the counter. "I watched it on YouTube."

He looked at me. "Do you want to know why I did it?"

I nodded. "I do. Amanda said something about anger management therapy. But you didn't look angry to me."

"That's because I wasn't," he said. "When we were growing up, Dex had this trick he'd pull whenever he got into a fight. He'd punch the other guy at exactly the right angle, hard enough that he'd make the guy's nose bleed with one shot. If you can do it, you've just gained the advantage in the fight. It's mostly over. Dex fights dirty, and he was a master at that move. He called it the Dexbleed."

I felt myself smirking.

"I know," Ryan said. "It's pretty good. Anyway, when we were fifteen, Dex offered to teach me how to do the Dexbleed. We went to the schoolyard after dinner and he taught me the whole thing. The angle you have to hit at, how to position your hand—everything. He showed me how to position your arm and your wrist, get power into it from your legs. It was fucking masterful." He sipped his juice, then put the glass down again. "We finished and we turned to leave. Then he turned back around and gave me a Dexbleed right in the face. It was a perfect shot. My nose bled like hell."

"Oh, my God," I said.

"I was pissed. I shouted at him, *What the fuck did you do that for?* And Dex said, *The most important part of the Dexbleed is surprise. That's the final lesson.*" He shifted his weight, leaning a hip against the counter. "It sounds like he's an asshole, and he is. But you know what? I used the Dexbleed to get out of every fight after that. That move saved me from getting the shit beat out of me more than once. And since I'd been on the receiving end, I knew how much it hurt. So in a weird way, Dex taught me something I needed to survive. And he was right. It only works when you surprise the other guy."

"It sounds like you grew up getting in a lot of fights," I said.

Ryan shrugged. "Everyone knew the Riggs brothers were badasses, so sooner or later most of them tried to take us on. But you can't use Dexbleeds in baseball.

"Anyway. One day I was on the field in the middle of a game, and I realized that I didn't want to be there. Dylan had the flu, and I'd had to leave him with a paid babysitter, and I was exhausted. I just didn't give a shit. And all of these guys, they take this game so fucking *seriously*. Like whoever hits the ball around a field is life and death. Baseball, to me, was a means to an end, and that was it. And Bennett Harding is talking to me about some play like it's so important, and I'm thinking, *This guy's name is Bennett Harding, and I haven't punched him for it. And I want to get off this field, out of this moment, and go see my kid. Right now. What would Dex do?*"

I bit my lip and waited.

Ryan shrugged. "So I gave him a Dexbleed. And they gave me a six-game suspension and sent me home."

I looked at his handsome face, his dark eyes so deep in thought. "Ryan," I said.

"I played one game after that," Ryan said. "Then my shoulder froze up so hard I could barely move. I haven't played another game to this day. And you know what? Last night I realized something. I played baseball for a while, and it was fine, but it was never really who I am. I'm a Riggs. *That's* who I am. It's my blood. You have to look at who you are, the good and the bad, and you have to face it or you're never going to get anywhere—that's what I think. And like it or not, Dex is my blood. He's more me than baseball ever was."

I couldn't say anything. There was a tight, breathless feeling in my chest.

Ryan looked away. "I guess that's a stupid story, right?"

I realized I'd been quiet so long I'd made him uncomfortable. "No," I said. "No, not at all. It's a great story."

"Yeah, well." He rinsed his glass and put it in the sink. "I have to go get Dylan before he has a panic attack. And you're going to be late for class."

He was right. I got ready, and I left the house and got in my car, heading for class. But the tight feeling never left my chest. I was almost all the way there before I figured out what it was.

Ryan was flawed and messed-up.

I still thought he was amazing.

I was completely in love with him.

And he had absolutely no idea at all.

WHEN I GOT home after classes, I could hear Ryan and Dylan in the living room upstairs. Dylan laughed about something, and then Ryan said something I couldn't hear—it sounded like a groan of pain—and then Dylan laughed again. I stood in the middle of my small apartment, listening to the happy trill of Dylan's laugh, and every cell of my body wanted to go upstairs. I didn't want to stay down here by myself, listening to them have fun. It suddenly seemed like the loneliest way in the world to pass the time.

I was still standing there, undecided and kind of sad, when Ryan said something to his son in a low voice and Dylan came thumping down the basement stairs. "Kate!" he said, knocking on my door. "Come up!"

I was already at the door before he got the words out. "Hi," I said.

He was basketball shorts and an oversized T-shirt, his dark hair in spikes like he hadn't combed it today—which he likely hadn't. "We got a new video game!" he said. "Come watch me and Dad!"

I followed him upstairs to find Ryan sprawled on the living room floor, pillows behind his shoulders and a game controller in his hand. His long, muscled body was gorgeous and relaxed, and his jaw was still scruffy. He glanced at me and smiled, making my knees turn to hot wax. "How were classes?"

"They were good," I said, taking a seat on the couch so I honestly couldn't stare at him. This was awkward, but it was still better than sitting downstairs by myself.

"Okay, well, Dyl and I are going to storm the castle and get the treasure, but we have to cross the river first."

"I know how to do it," Dylan said, sitting next to his father and picking up his own controller. "There's a boat downstream, remember? We have to steal it."

I watched them for a few minutes. It seemed to be a team-playing game in which Ryan and Dylan worked together instead of competing. It was a medieval setting, and they were both knights who had to get into a castle. It was long on strategy, low on violence. Dylan was already totally into it.

"If we steal the boat, we'll wake him up," Ryan said as the two knights circled a sleeping guard.

"Should we swim?" Dylan asked.

"We have armor on. We'll sink."

"What does this do?" Dylan moved his knight to a wooden plank and shoved it, revealing a gleam of gold. "I found coins!"

"Nice going," Ryan said. "Maybe if we find more money we can buy the boat off him?"

"No, look," I said, chiming in. "There's a rope. Over next to that barrel. See? I bet you can pull it and steal the boat without the guard waking up."

We sat like that for a while, talking and playing. Ryan gave me his controller while he went to the kitchen to pop popcorn, and I took over being a knight alongside Dylan. When Ryan came back I gave the controller back, not because I didn't want to play, but because I really wanted the popcorn. So I curled up on the couch and ate and we played some more.

I want this, I thought. *Just this. Hanging out with these two, being a part of this.*

I remembered Lauren's words: *You can be his nanny, or you can date him. You can't do both.* She was right, I realized. And now I knew which one I wanted. I didn't want to be the nanny anymore, the paid help. I wanted to belong here because they wanted me. Because Ryan wanted me.

So, I decided: I'd get Ryan alone later, after Dylan was in bed. I'd give my notice. And I'd ask him if he wanted to go out with me. For real—a date.

He might say no. But I'd felt how he touched me, how he'd curled himself around me that first night we were in his bed. I had a feeling he might say yes.

I'd said just last night that I wasn't ready, but what if I could make it work? What if Ryan and I took it slow while I went to school? How would we broach it with Dylan? There was no script, no set of instructions to follow for us. We'd have to make it up. But what if we tried? What could we do if we both wanted it badly enough?

I was silently hyperventilating on the sofa, watching them play with my stomach in knots, when the doorbell rang.

Ryan paused the game and frowned. "What the hell?"

"I can get it," Dylan said.

Ryan aimed his frown at his son. "No way. What did I tell you about answering the door?"

"I'll get it," I said. I got up and walked to the front door, pulling it open.

A woman stood there. She was about my age, tall and willowy, wearing hip-hugging jeans, a dark sweater, a leather jacket, and low-heeled boots. Her hair was caramel-colored, in long, loose curls flowing over her shoulders. Her eyes were dark brown and somehow slightly familiar. She wore very little makeup, but she didn't need it because she was naturally, ravishingly beautiful.

She looked a little surprised to see me, but then she smiled politely. "Oh, hi," she said. "I'm here to see Ryan."

I was so surprised I had no words. "I'm sorry?"

"Is he here? I need to talk to him."

I looked at her again and my stomach fell. Dropped down, down, down. Because I knew why I recognized those eyes. And I knew what she was about to say before she said it.

"My name's Amber," the woman said. "I'm Dylan's mother. And if he's here, I'd like to see him too."

TWENTY-THREE

Ryan

THIS WAS NOT HAPPENING. This was not fucking happening.

I hadn't heard that voice in eight years. To be honest, I hadn't heard it very much at all. Just some drunken conversation at a party, and then her moaning in my ear. And now: "I'm Dylan's mother. And if he's here, I'd like to see him too."

My kid went pale and his eyes went wide. I leapt up from the floor and walked to the front door. There was Amber, looking the same as she had the night I knocked her up, except a little older. She looked at me and smiled like we were friends. Like I should be fucking happy.

"What do you think you're doing?" I said to her. "You can't just show up here."

Amber's smile faded. I was seeing red. I didn't care about me, or about anyone. But this woman had just dropped a bomb on Dylan, and I had no idea how he would take it.

A hand touched my wrist, quickly and gently. Kate. She was reminding me that losing my temper and shouting wasn't going to make this go over better with Dylan. I took a breath. "You need to leave," I said to Amber.

"He's my son," she said. "Is he—Oh, my God." Her eyes went wide. She was looking past me, and I knew who was standing behind me.

"Dad?" Dylan said.

Oh, Jesus. This was the worst thing that could happen. I had never thought about how Dylan would meet his mother, because she was always on the other side of the planet, doing whatever stupid shit she did to avoid her responsibilities. I hadn't prepared him. I hadn't talked to her about it—I hadn't talked to her at all. Amber was gone, and Dylan was mine. That was as far as I'd planned it.

Now I realized that was a mistake. I hadn't been vigilant enough. I should have thought that this could get sprung on him without warning. But now it was too late.

"Dylan!" Amber pushed past me and Kate and knelt in front of him. When they were face to face, I could see the ways he looked like her, just like I could see how he looked like me when we stood in front of a mirror together. She put her arms around him and hugged him tight. He looked stunned. I knew the feeling.

Amber pulled back, though she didn't let him go. "I'm your mother," she said, smiling like this was all a happy reunion. "I've been away for a while, but now I'm back! What do you think?"

"I don't know," Dylan said in a small voice.

"You're so big!" she said sweetly. "And so handsome! Oh, my goodness. What a wonderful boy you are! I'm so happy!"

Dylan was getting that look on his face, like he was about to puke. I wouldn't be surprised if, in his seven-year-old mind, he thought I'd tell him to pack his bags and go live with this strange woman from now on.

"Why are you here?" he asked her.

"Because I'm back now," Amber said. "I want to be friends with you. Does that sound like fun?"

I had to do something. I couldn't shout at her, and I couldn't move in and physically pull her off him—both of those would freak him out. So I stood next to Dylan and touched the top of his head. "I'm sorry about this, dude," I said to him. "I had no idea she was coming. I would have warned you. I'm gonna tell her to leave and come back some other time."

Amber let him go, offended. Dylan moved closer to my leg. "It's okay," he said, being polite. This fucking kid. I'd never seen anyone try so hard.

I touched his head again in reassurance. "Amber," I said, "Come back some other time."

She stood from where she was crouched on the floor. "He's my son," she said. She glanced briefly at Kate, dismissing her, then looked back at me. "Ryan, he's *our* son."

Something cold crept down my spine. That was a coded message, and I had no idea what it meant. I had no idea what Amber's play was. I didn't know her at all.

What did she want? Money? Custody? Or was she really just this stupid?

I needed intel. "All right," I said to her. "Why don't you and I go talk for a while? Just us. There's a place up the street we can go."

That surprised her. She thought it over, shot another glance Kate's way. Then she turned back to me and smiled. I remembered that she was good-looking, which was what I'd thought at nineteen. She probably thought her looks were helping her now.

"Okay," she said. "Let's go."

I grabbed my coat and turned to Kate. I had to get Amber the hell out of here. "Sorry," I said. "Can you hold the fort for a little while?"

"Sure," she said. Her face was blank, like a canvas with nothing painted on it. Her voice was flat.

I paused. "Kate?"

Her gaze met mine, and something flashed there, something that looked a lot like pain. "Go," she said, her voice harsh. "Everything is fine here. Go."

Fuck. I'd done something wrong. I had no idea what it was. I had no idea what was the right option in this situation. But I had to work this out. I had to go.

So I did the last thing I wanted to do, now or ever.

I turned back to Amber, and I left.

THE PLACE down the street was a dingy pub, and Amber didn't want to go there, so we had to get in my SUV and find somewhere else. We ended up at the Fire Pit, which was Westlake's teen hangout, serving sandwiches and no alcohol. I'd spent my share of time here while I went to Westlake High, picking up girls a million years ago. At nine o'clock on a Saturday night there were gaggles of teens in here, tall lanky dudes with cracking voices and giggling girls. But Amber didn't want to go anywhere that served alcohol, so we took a booth and sat down.

She smiled at me again. I racked my brain trying to remember what I knew about her. She'd gone to Westlake High, but I'd never even talked to her until that night at the party. I'd never tried, because in those days I always had plenty of girls to talk to. Amber was just one of a long line.

Fuck, I didn't even remember what we talked about that night. It was all a blur. I didn't usually drink that hard, but my team had just won a big game. Amber and I had ended up in a bathroom, and we'd fucked against the sink while someone pounded on the door. We'd both thought it was funny.

That moment had led directly to this one, eight years later. You make your decisions and you live with them.

"You look good, Ryan," she said.

I didn't say anything. The waitress brought us a couple of Cokes, which we didn't touch.

"I suppose you'd like to know where I've been," Amber said. "I'm sorry I've been absent. The fact is, I've been on a spiritual journey."

"No," I said. "You've been in Thailand with some guy, according to your parents."

She sighed. "I've been trying to find myself. I just felt... constricted here. Penned in. Like I couldn't breathe."

"So you goofed off for seven years."

"I was an unformed spirit back then." She said this with deadly seriousness, as if this was an actual thing people say to each other. "I needed to search for my truth. Haven't you ever wanted to search for your truth?"

"No," I said honestly. "I've been too busy making sure Dylan got fed and not nabbed by a serial killer. That's pretty much all I do."

"The east is so much more enlightened than here," Amber said. "You can truly center yourself there in a way you can't in our society. It's been so jarring, being back in the States. You can't even *think* here."

"So why did you come back?"

She traced a finger through the sweat on her Coke glass. "I realized that part of my truth is that I'm a mother. I'm connected with the One Mother, the oneness of womanhood. And to deny that truth was causing me pain. So I've come back to embrace it. To embrace the motherhood within me."

It was like she was speaking another language. She couldn't possibly be this dense. "He's a kid, not a concept," I said. "What are you saying, Amber? Are you saying you want our kid?"

It wasn't going to happen. One of the things I'd done, not long after Dylan landed on my doorstep, was make him fully, legally mine. I'd done it on Wes's advice, because at the time I wasn't sure that Amber's parents wouldn't try to take him back. Her parents had a lot of money, which was why Amber could afford to do fuck all with herself on their dime. I didn't want them hiring lawyers and taking Dylan back.

So I petitioned for full custody, which they didn't contest. Amber didn't contest it either, so custody went to me. She had no play in this game.

I wondered if she'd get lawyers. After seven years away, she'd have a fuck of a lot to prove in order to get anywhere. And it would be very, very expensive. Then again, maybe the parents would pay, like they paid for everything.

"I don't want to fight, Ryan," Amber said.

"Good, because you won't win."

"This is already feeling very confrontational," she said. "I sense a lot of defensiveness coming from you. And anger. It's negative energy. It's so unhealthy."

"I'm defensive because you showed up on my doorstep and upset my kid," I said. "How do you not see that?"

"Our child," she corrected me. "We made him together."

"We fucked in a bathroom, you mean."

For a second her pupils dilated. "Crudeness is another form of defense," she said, her voice softer.

I leaned forward. "Cut the crap, Amber. What's your play?"

Her pupils were still dark, and her gaze was still fixed on me. "I want what's best for Dylan," she said.

"Which is?"

"Both his parents."

I stared at her for a long minute. Was she saying what I thought she was saying? After eight years?

"You can't possibly be serious," I said.

She bit her lip. "That woman. The one back at your house. Who is she? My parents said you weren't married."

Now I was starting to see red again. "She's none of your business."

"But she's not your wife."

I narrowed my eyes at her and didn't answer.

"It's a circle, Ryan," Amber said. "A sacred circle. The male and the female powers combine to create life. The child flourishes best under the influence of both the yoni and the lingam. The ones who created him. Me and you."

I closed my eyes for a second. I had a headache, and pain was crawling up my shoulder and down my back for the first time in weeks. "Amber," I said slowly, "I can't believe I'm saying this, but I could not be less interested in your yoni if I tried. And you are never getting anywhere near my lingam ever again."

She licked her lip, uncertain. She had nice lips, I'd give her that. At nineteen, that move would have given me a boner. At twenty-seven, I just wanted her to go away. "Could we at least try?" she said.

And then it clicked. All this shit about her yoni and the rest of it—it was exactly that, bullshit. We'd known each other for a drunken hour eight years ago. And I may be good-looking, but I wasn't so fucking amazing that a woman would cross the planet after eight years just to get into bed with me.

She wanted access to Dylan. For whatever reason, after all this time she wanted to get near him, and she couldn't because she had no rights. She could probably hire lawyers, but why bother doing it the hard way when you can do it the easy way—get slutty Ryan Riggs to start fucking you again?

After all, I had no standards, right? I'd fuck anything that moved. So she gets me into bed, and she gets everything she wants without a fight. And—judging by the look in her eye and the body language she was giving me right now—the good girl gets to have a few orgasms with the bad boy in the process. She gets convenient dirty sex while pretending to be above it all, more spiritual than me. Sex and rebellion had always been my specialties.

Like Kate, whose only compliment to me was *You are so sexy.* No matter what I did or how hard I tried. *You are so sexy.*

And suddenly I was tired. Very fucking tired. I had a bad shoulder and a kid to raise and calluses on my hands from working with them all day, and this woman wanted a guilt-free fuck so she could get what she wanted. Which was access to my son. Kate said I should respect myself; I was about to start now.

"This act," I said to Amber. "Does it get you a lot of dick?"

She blinked at me, shocked.

"Yeah, I bet it does." I answered my own question. "This spiritual act of yours. I bet guys fall for it like dominoes. Well, here's the deal: You're not a mother. Giving birth to Dylan doesn't make you his mother. Got it?"

"Ryan—"

"He had a stomach bug last week," I said, interrupting her. "He drank grape juice, and then he puked it all up. He tried to get to the toilet but he didn't make it. I cleaned for an hour, and I was still finding bright purple chunks of puke the next day. He tried to go to school and he puked on the driveway, and I had to get out the hose. Where were you?"

She went pale and didn't answer.

"Right," I said. "He has nightmares. He gets sick. He thinks fart jokes are the height of humor. He can be stubborn and pissy. He's in tears over multiplication tables. And you're in Thailand, meditating over your yoni. It doesn't work that way." I stood up. "If you want to see him, get your lawyer to draw up a petition for visitation. My lawyer will let you know if I agree or not. And do not fucking come to my door again."

I left, and I got in my car, but I didn't go home. I couldn't. I was still mad, and I didn't want Dylan to see me this way. I felt like someone had doused gasoline over my right shoulder and lit a match, the pain burning down my back. And I couldn't help but remember that when Dylan had been upset over his multiplication tables, it wasn't me that helped him with it. It was Kate.

Kate, who didn't want me.

I wanted her. And if she didn't want me back, then the only thing I wanted was those fucking white pills.

I turned the key and started driving.

TWENTY-FOUR

Kate

I HEARD the front door open upstairs. I opened my eyes in the dark and rolled over in bed. I was lying on top of the covers, still fully dressed, as I'd been when I lay down a few hours ago. I blinked, disoriented, listening to Ryan's quiet footsteps in the hall.

For the second night in a row, I followed the sound of his footsteps into the living room, then the hallway, then as they receded up the stairs.

I'd sat with Dylan until he fell asleep. He was confused and tired, his emotions in a jumble after the sudden appearance of his mother. I had no idea what to do, so I'd walked him through his bedtime routine, hoping something would come to me. Then I'd read *Harry Potter* to him while he lay in bed. It took him a long time to drift off, but he finally did it.

When will Dad be back? Dylan had asked. And I'd said *Soon.*
It wasn't a good answer, but it was the only one I knew. Because I
had no idea where Ryan had gone, or what was taking him so
long to come home.

I rolled over and found my phone on my bedside table in the
dark. I touched it and looked at the time. It was two thirty in the
morning.

I stared at those numbers, feeling like someone had punched
me in the stomach. Feeling everything drain out of me, leaving
nothing left.

He'd left with Amber. He'd said they were going to talk. And
he came home at two thirty in the morning.

He'd been angry with her. He hadn't wanted to talk to her, I
knew that—he'd made the suggestion just to get her out of the
house without shouting at her in front of Dylan. I didn't like
watching them leave, but I'd told myself that it was for Dylan's
sake, and that if Amber was back from wherever she'd been, he
was going to have to talk to her sometime. He may as well get it
over with now.

And then he'd stayed out with her for over six hours.

The pain surprised me. The suddenness of it and the force of
it. It took my breath away, thinking of Ryan with her all night.
She was beautiful and sexy, and she was Dylan's mother. And
she wanted Ryan—she'd made that clear, at least to me. Maybe it
was an impulse of hers when she saw him, or maybe she'd carried
a torch for him all this time. I didn't know which one it was, but I
knew that Amber wasn't back just for conversation. She wanted
all of it—the man, the boy, everything. The package deal.

And what was I? The nanny, the sometime fuck. I wasn't
Ryan's wife or even his girlfriend; I was the paid help, the one
who found him convenient to sleep with. It would be easy to
sweep me aside, calculate me out of the equation. A smart

woman, a sexy woman, one who had a deep and irrevocable claim on Ryan, could do just that.

She could try, at least. All Ryan had to do was say no and come home. But he hadn't.

Whatever they'd done, he'd said yes to—for hours. Whether it was talking or fucking or something else, he'd said yes to it while I sat home alone, wondering where he was.

I rolled over and sat up on the side of the bed. I rubbed my face and realized my cheeks were wet with tears. "I'm not doing this," I said out loud.

The words hurt, so I said them again. "I'm not doing this."

You can be his nanny, or you can date him. You can't do both. Actually, I couldn't do either. I already wasn't dating him. And I couldn't be his nanny while Dylan's mother worked her way back into the picture. I couldn't watch that, and if Ryan expected me to, then he wasn't the man I'd thought he was.

Then again, if he'd just spent the night in bed with Amber, then he already wasn't the man I'd thought he was.

I stood up. I was too tired to think about this. The night's events had exhausted me, and I couldn't think straight. It was technically Sunday, my day off, and I couldn't spend it sitting in my little apartment, listening to Ryan and Dylan overhead. The idea was torture.

I switched on the bedside lamp and put my glasses on. I pulled a bag out of the closet. I packed some clothes, some toiletries, my notebooks and textbooks. My laptop. I tied my hair in a knot and found my sweater, my coat, my boots.

I sat for a long minute, listening to the silence of the house. Wondering if Ryan was awake, or if he'd fallen asleep already. Wondering if he was thinking about me at all.

But no. I needed to think about myself, not him. "I'm not doing this," I said one more time, this time a whisper. I stood up and picked up my bag.

I should leave. Just go. But I thought of Dylan and I couldn't quite do it. So I found a piece of paper and wrote him a note. *Going away for a few days. Be back soon. Kate.*

I tiptoed upstairs and found Dylan's backpack, the one he could never find. I put the note in the pocket. Only one I had done that could I finally walk out the door.

I FOUND A HOTEL DOWNTOWN, the kind of hotel business travelers came to for meetings and PowerPoint presentations. I couldn't stay here forever, but I could afford a few days. I slept for a while, and after the sun came up I showered and went out for a drive.

I didn't know what I was doing. I had no plan. But this was what I needed: quiet in my head, in my heart. Quiet to think about myself and what I wanted and nothing else.

Just after eight, my phone rang. It was Ryan. I sent it to voicemail, and he sent a string of texts instead, because he knew I was ignoring him.

Kate

Where the fuck are you

You aren't downstairs

Kate??

Tell me you're okay before I lose my shit

I pulled into the parking lot of a breakfast place. I texted him back. *I'm fine. I'm just taking some time. Some space.*

The phone rang again, and I sent it to voicemail again. I couldn't talk to him. I couldn't.

The string of texts started again.

Shit I did something, right?

What was it

Tell me

That was like a stab to the chest. I felt like shouting at him: *You don't fucking know? You stayed out with your ex until two thirty in the morning and you don't fucking know?*

But I had no heart for a fight right now. I was too tired and confused and heartsick. I didn't want shouting and recriminations. I wanted peace.

I'm turning my phone off now, I wrote.

I didn't see what he wrote after that. I pressed the power button and watched my phone shut down.

I'd grown up in the suburbs of Detroit, where everyone said the nice people still lived. The people in my neighborhood growing up had money, though they never struck me as particularly nice. Or particularly happy.

Westlake was different. It was smaller, but it wasn't a small town. The downtown had a few office buildings and parking lots and a mall that had been partly demolished and reworked as an open-air shopping space, plus a newer mall near Riggs Auto Two. It was half an hour's drive to woods and beaches, so there were vacation places. And of course it had the railroad tracks. One side was where the nice people lived, and the other side was where the Riggs brothers lived. Where I lived.

I drove until I found a sign that said Pike's Point, and I followed it. Pike's Point turned out not to be a point at all—it was just a grassy stretch of land surrounded by trees, with the cold gray of water beyond. Now, in October, the trees were stripped of leaves, the ground was dirty brown, and the sky was chilly. There was no one here. I got out my laptop and sat at a picnic table, winding a scarf around my neck.

There was no wifi, but it didn't matter. I'd downloaded a week's worth of exercises for my course, and I worked on them for a while, getting my textbook out of the car and reading a few of the lessons. Then, with inspiration tickling the back of my mind, I opened a blank document and started typing ideas.

Forty-five minutes later I had brainstormed two pages, filled with bullet points, dates, dollar signs, and question marks. My fingers were numb and my nose and cheeks were cold, but I felt an excitement I'd never felt before. Like I had something at my fingertips that I could really want. That I could actually do.

I brought my laptop back to the car and dumped it in the passenger seat. In the driver's seat, I picked up my phone and powered it on again, steeling myself for what I might find.

But the phone powered up, and all the little icons appeared, and nothing. Not a text, not a phone call had come in. Nothing at all.

So Ryan hadn't responded at all after my last text. I felt a slow burn of pain at that. He had nothing to say.

Then again, what had I expected? I'd told him I was turning my phone off. Did I want him to sit there, calling and texting me while I didn't answer?

I scrolled through the numbers on my phone. I had been given everyone's number, because I had to have all of the emergency contacts. Because I was the nanny.

Or maybe I wasn't the nanny anymore.

Ignoring the way the pain blossomed at that, I dialed one of the numbers. A familiar woman's voice answered. "Hello?"

"Lauren, it's Kate."

"Hey, Kate. What's up?"

"I have a question."

"Go ahead."

I had to square my shoulders, as if I was in a job interview. "If I was going to start a business, would you help me out?"

"Yes."

"I don't mean money or anything. I'd get a loan from the bank. But I could use your advice on how to do all of that. Where to start."

"Yes."

"I'll try not to take up a lot of your time. And I know you're burned out and everything, but—"

"Yes, Kate," Lauren said. "I'll help you start a business. In fact, I'd love to. I think it would be fun."

"You don't even know what kind of business it is."

"Do I have to know?"

I thought about that. "Well, I think it's a good idea. And I think it could work. I have a few different locations in mind—"

"We'll go location scouting," Lauren said. She wasn't bossy or controlling, just decisive. Confident. I felt my own confidence growing, just listening to her talk about this like it was no big deal. "We can go sometime this week and you can tell me all about it, show me what locations you're thinking of. When are you free? Are you available during the day while Dylan is in school?"

My confidence fumbled. I couldn't tell her that I wasn't living at Ryan's, at least not right now. "Um, yes," I said. "I have a class tomorrow, but I can do Tuesday."

"Tuesday," Lauren said. "Come to my place at, say ten? I'll text you the address."

I agreed, and after I hung up I sat there, trying to breathe. I could have used a paper bag to breathe into. Then I looked at my phone again and saw no messages from Ryan, and felt like crying. I was going insane.

So I scrolled through my contacts again and found another one. I hit Call.

"Hi, Kate."

Tara's voice was calm and friendly. I immediately felt better.

"Are you busy?" I asked her. Sunday was her day off, but I had no idea what she did on her weekends. Probably banged Jace nonstop. I couldn't blame her.

But she heard something in my voice, because she said, "No, I'm not busy. What do you need to talk about?"

That was all I needed. The words started coming, and I let them. I talked and talked. I told her everything, about me and Ryan, about five years ago, about the sex, about how I felt last night and what I had been planning to do. I told her about Amber showing up, about Ryan leaving with her and not coming back. I told her about this morning, the hotel, sitting in Pike's Park by myself in the cold, feeling good and terrible at the same time. I told her everything.

Tara didn't freak out. She didn't even say *Wow* or *OMG*. She just said, "Okay. First of all, I think you've done the right thing, at least for now."

I felt something loosen in me, like an elastic that had been twisted too tight. "You do?"

"Yes. It's obvious that your situation is difficult right now. You're living in Ryan's house, and you're his employee. You're also sleeping with him and you have feelings for him, and at the same time you're taking a course and trying to start your career. And now Dylan's mother has showed up. No wonder you're confused. If I were your counselor, I'd advise you to remove yourself physically from the situation, at least for a little while. You can't make good decisions while you're in the middle of it."

I slumped into my seat as she talked. "Part of me feels like a heel," I said.

"I think you need to give notice," Tara said thoughtfully. "I don't think it's possible for you to be his employee anymore. As for the rest of it, the two of you are going to have to figure it out. You'll have to communicate."

I knew what she was saying. "You mean I have to talk to him. I can't avoid him forever."

"Well, yes. Talking is really the best thing to do. But your emotions are running high since this woman showed up."

I closed my eyes and said the thing that scared me. "She's Dylan's mother. Isn't it best if he has his mother in his life? If they raise him together? That at least means she's going to be around, right?"

"Not necessarily," Tara said. "Custody is very complicated, and she gave Dylan up at birth. She hasn't proven herself capable of being a good mother. But I'm not a judge. The short answer is yes, if she's very determined and has money for a lawyer, then she will be around."

Tall, beautiful Amber, with her long flowing hair and her perfect lips. "She was interested in starting something with him. Romantically." She'd practically shouted it at me: *Back off, I'm back now, get out.* Maybe Ryan couldn't see it, but I could.

"Maybe," Tara said, skeptical. "It seems to me that if she's been carrying a torch for Ryan, we would have heard from her before now. She might just be looking for an easy way to get to Dylan."

I hadn't thought of that. It *was* weird that Amber would show up after eight years to get Ryan straight into bed on the first night. I'd chalked it up to their being attracted to each other, to both of them being gorgeous. To the fact that they'd made a baby together. I was looking at it through the lens of hurt and—I could admit it—total, rabid jealousy.

But maybe Amber didn't really want Ryan. Maybe that night eight years ago was as meaningless to her as it seemed to be to him. I'd had my own night with Ryan, which had lasted a lot longer than Amber's, and though I'd really enjoyed it, I hadn't been heartbroken afterward. I hadn't called him and followed him around. I'd just shaken it off and moved on. Ryan Riggs, the player, was the kind of guy you did that with: had great sex, then moved on. Right?

That was the man Amber knew. That was the man she probably assumed she was coming back to. The guy who would drop his pants at the first invitation, especially from a beautiful woman. The guy whose feelings, if he even had them, didn't matter.

He'd been a player, and he certainly had treated women that way, at least for a while. But the truth was, the women had treated him the same way, too. I had. Amber had. And now she was treating him the same way again.

Was I?

I'd left, and I'd told him I was turning my phone off. For the first time, it occurred to me that he might not be pissed at me. He might be hurt instead.

"If she's after Dylan after all this time, then she's a bitch," I said, because it was easier to be angry at Amber than at myself.

"Well, she's certainly selfish," Tara said. "She's already shown that she isn't putting Dylan first. So, yes, she is a bit of a bitch."

I laughed. She was so totally a counselor. I could see why she was good at her job.

"Here's my personal advice," Tara said. "I don't know Ryan all that well, but I think it's really unlikely anything happened with Amber last night. This is hard on him, Kate. Even harder than it is on you. He's built a life for Dylan out of almost nothing, it's taken him years, and Amber is threatening it. I personally think she's the last person he'd jump into bed with."

"Okay," I said.

"Also, I saw the way he looked at you when we were at Luke and Emily's engagement party. He rather adores you, you know."

I closed my eyes and scrubbed a hand through my hair. "That's insane."

"Why? Because he's handsome? So what? You're the only woman he's been interested in in years, honey. Years. You should own that. Jace is my person, my favorite person, and we're weirdly perfect for each other, but he's also hot. And believe me, I enjoy every minute of it."

"Tara," I said, "if he doesn't marry you, then I will."

She laughed. "Thanks, but you're not my type. Keep me posted, okay? Good luck."

TWENTY-FIVE

Ryan

BY THE THIRD DAY, things were falling apart at my house. I had to take Dylan to school and back, which meant I went in late to Riggs Auto Two and left early. The fridge emptied, the clutter piled up, the laundry was everywhere. Kate had kept her word and had never done the work of a housekeeper, but I realized now that when she was around, Dylan and I were neater. We tried harder. Now she was gone and we were both miserable.

Dylan was confused and moody after the reappearance of his mother and Kate's leaving. Sometimes he was my son, and sometimes he was this strange alien boy I didn't recognize. He asked me questions I didn't know the answers to. His appetite went down. He freaked out over a slice of apple, and I couldn't even get too mad at him. He was stressed out. I knew the feeling.

I couldn't feel much of anything. I was hollowed-out and

empty without Kate. I wished I wasn't—I wished I could just write the whole thing off and not care. Instead I felt like someone had pried open my rib cage and scraped everything out of me, put it in a bucket, and walked away. My stomach had an ache low in the pit of it, like dread. My shoulder burned. Sleep was a joke. Twice I picked up the phone to make the call to get myself some pills, and twice I put it down again.

The dialogue in my head was always the same. *She doesn't want you, loser. She never did. You were a job and a good fuck, that's all. What woman would want in on the shit show that is your life?*

It was the only conclusion I had. Amber had showed up once, and Kate had packed her bags in the middle of the night, turned her phone off, and not contacted me again. *Oh well, things got hard, time to go.* You don't stick around to help the guy who's your occasional fuck with lawyer appointments and custody shit. Kate hadn't signed up for that. She was out.

I would be mad, if I could feel anything except the drained, awful feeling of missing her.

"I have to go soon," I told Dex as we finished up a job at Riggs Auto Two. It was after two, and I had to go pick up Dylan. I had an alarm set on my phone so I wouldn't be late.

Surprisingly, Dex didn't give me shit. In fact, he hadn't given me shit all week—not when I came in late or left early, not on Monday when I brought Dylan to the shop with me after school so we wouldn't get behind. He just grunted and nodded and did the work that needed doing. It wasn't much like Dex, but I wasn't about to ask questions.

I checked my phone, then shoved it back in my pocket and found that Dex was looking at me. We were on either side of the hood of a car, and he was wiping his hands slowly with a rag.

"You need the name of a good lawyer?" he asked. "I know a few."

Another surprise. I shook my head. "I've got it covered, thanks." I already had a good lawyer—the one who'd drawn up my custody papers in the first place. I'd called him and told him what had happened with Amber. His advice was not to contact her and not to talk to her if she showed up again—basically, not to do a fucking thing. That was fine with me.

Dex scratched his chin, thinking. "You want my guess?" he said. "She'll fuck off and go back to Thailand."

I'd told him the bare basics of what had gone on with Amber. Not because Dex was that great a confidant, but because I wanted him to know in case Amber ever came to Riggs Auto Two looking for Dylan. "Do you know any scary guys who might convince her?" I said, trying for a joke.

"Yes," Dex said, deadpan. "But I won't call them. I won't need to. She'll fuck this up on her own."

"How do you know that?"

"Because she's an idiot," Dex said, as if this were obvious.

I looked away. That was kind of funny, but I didn't feel like laughing.

"I got a call from a guy," Dex said. "He sells to all the athletes in Detroit. He wanted me to find out if you still wanted those pills you were taking."

I actually felt lightheaded. I had to put my hand on the car in front of me. I didn't need anyone knowing that shit, but of all people, I didn't want Dex knowing it. "He's lying," I said.

"No, he isn't," Dex said.

"Why did he call you?"

"Because he has product to move, and you haven't answered any of his texts in months. You blocked him. He thinks you got another supplier."

"And you know this guy?"

"I know a lot of people," Dex said. "It doesn't mean I like them, it just means I know them."

I thought about Dex, about why he wasn't a cop anymore. Some rumors said he had a nervous breakdown and couldn't hack it, and other rumors said that he got out before he could be hit with corruption charges. The problem with Dex was that either one could be true—or neither. You never knew with him.

"You need to get better friends," I told him.

"I don't have any friends," Dex said.

"I'm not taking them anymore. The pills, I mean. I stopped a while ago."

Dex nodded. "You feel like taking them now?"

There was no point in denying it. He already knew. "All the time. But I won't."

"You better not," my brother said. "Let me tell you something, Riggs. If you score—no matter who it's from or where—I'll know about it. And I'll kick your teeth in. You'll hurt so bad the Dexbleed will seem like a picnic. Now go get your kid and get out of here."

LATE THAT NIGHT I was lying in bed, staring at the ceiling. Dylan was asleep in his room, but as usual my thoughts wouldn't shut up. My head was buzzing with lack of sleep, but my body didn't get the message. So I lay there as the two of them battled it out.

On the nightstand, my phone vibrated. I made myself wait a long moment before I picked it up. *That isn't a text from Kate,* I reminded myself. *You think it is, but it isn't.*

I finally picked up the phone and let myself look. I felt a jolt of energy go through me when I saw Kate's name.

Hey, she wrote. *I have to pick up a few of my things tomorrow. Just letting you know.*

The empty space in my ribcage hollowed out a little more. I couldn't let her get off that easy. *That's it, then?* I wrote back. *We're done?*

There was a long pause, and I thought she'd turned her phone off again. Then the dots moved.

We need to talk, she wrote, *but I need some time. I'm very confused.*

Welcome to the club, I texted back.

I don't think I'm handling this very well, she wrote.

I scrubbed a hand over my face. The pain in my shoulder was nothing compared to the other pain I felt right now. Was this what it felt like to be in love with someone? How the fuck did anyone stand it? I wanted her back, but I couldn't have her. Sure, I could track her down, make some big gesture, and maybe get her into bed—but that would be all it was. I knew that. It would just be killing time until she left again. I didn't have some magical dick that could make a woman love me when she didn't already. I wished I did, but I didn't.

I could find her. I could try and convince her. But we'd seen each other every day for months, and we'd lived in the same house for weeks now. We'd talked and we'd had sex and she knew everything about me. If she wasn't convinced, I had no idea what would do it.

Okay, I texted her. *I'll look for another nanny.* Because I couldn't do this shit by myself. I had no idea how I'd done it as long as I had. No wonder I was cracking up by the time Kate came to my doorstep.

I'd find someone else. I'd go to an agency or something. I'd get someone who I didn't have a history with, who was in the business of taking care of kids. Someone who definitely would not live in my house and make me insane.

You should find someone, Kate wrote. *I'm sorry.*

Everyone is fucking sorry, I wrote back. *I'm turning my phone off now.*

And I did it. I turned my phone off and put it down.

It was still a long time before I closed my eyes.

TWENTY-SIX

Kate

JUST A FEW MORE DAYS. That was what I'd convinced myself I needed: a few more days to think things over and sort them through.

I'd spent the past few days keeping busy. I went to class and did my homework. I spent Tuesday driving around Westlake with Lauren, telling her about my business idea and looking at possible locations. She said my idea was a good one, and we checked out the competition, which turned out to be scarce in Westlake. That only made my idea seem stronger.

I read books. I talked to my parents. But at night I sat alone in my hotel room, thinking about Ryan and Dylan and wondering what they were doing. Wondering if they missed me. Wondering if they were okay.

I ran out of clean clothes, so I had to text Ryan to tell him I was going to pick up some of my things. To say sorry. *Everyone is fucking sorry,* he wrote, and I realized I'd hurt him. Maybe permanently. And I didn't know what to do.

Even when I'd had a boyfriend everyone expected me to marry, it hadn't been this hard. I'd decided that Mark wasn't someone I wanted to spend my life with, and I'd broken it off. I was twenty-one, and at the time I thought it was the worst thing I'd ever go through. In fact, it was a little bit uncomfortable, and that was it.

This was different. I thought about Ryan constantly. I wanted to know what he was doing, what he was thinking. I wanted to talk to him. My body missed him like crazy, especially at night when I got into bed alone.

There was no one at the house when I got there. I went around back and entered my basement apartment, grabbing some clothes and a few of the toiletries I'd forgotten. I tried not to linger, because I liked my little apartment—I'd made it my own space, filled with things I liked. I spent as little time as possible in the bedroom, where Ryan had visited me and we'd made each other crazy. I tried not to look at the bed, which was still rumpled from when I'd slept in it last.

When I finished, I walked to the basement door and I paused. I'd left a few things upstairs—a sweater, a textbook I needed. I could maybe tell Ryan to collect them for me, but that would be even more cowardly than I already was. I turned the knob and climbed the stairs.

I stepped into the living room, and the breath left my chest.

To anyone else, it looked like a messy living room—toys, games, clothes everywhere. It looked a lot like the living room I'd seen that first day I'd come for an interview. Because Ryan and Dylan lived here. They didn't just use this space, they lived in it.

I took a step in and looked around. Dylan's baseball jersey was crumpled up at the end of the sofa—baseball season was almost over, and he was outgrowing this jersey. He needed a new one by next season, and this one needed a washing. The video game controllers were put away—it looked like they weren't playing the medieval knight game anymore. I wondered if they ever got to the castle.

In the kitchen, one of Dylan's schoolbooks was on the kitchen table. It was the workbook of math problems, and next to it was a stack of papers with Dylan's big handwriting on them, trying to figure them out. Next to that was another stack of papers—this one in Ryan's bold, hard writing. I picked up the top sheet and read it. Ryan had sat with his son and tried to work through the same math problems, probably to see if they'd come up with the same answer.

The fridge was nearly empty, the front of it covered in post-it notes: *Buy milk. Lettuce. Cheese.* A note in Dylan's careful scrawl: *Dylan hair cut Friday.* Another one: *Fix bike tire!!!*

Everything—every tiny, inconsequential thing—hit me like a blow. I put my hands on my stomach, like someone was punching me, and I started to cry.

These were my guys. This was their life. When had this ever been a job to me? I couldn't remember. I could only remember both of them being my life.

I mopped my face and pulled out my phone. I wandered back to the staircase leading upstairs and sat on a step, trying to get myself together. At the bottom of the stairs were Dylan's shoes, Ryan's trainers. A post-it note on the wall above the hook said *Dylan's backpack goes here!!*

I swiped my phone on and called Ryan.

He answered right away. "Kate?"

I thought I could talk, but at the sound of his voice I couldn't. I sniffed instead.

Now he was alarmed. "*Kate?*"

"I'm at the house." I sniffed again. "I don't want to leave."

"Jesus," he said softly, and the word sounded pained.

"Dylan's math answers are right," I said, wiping my cheeks. "The ones I saw, anyway. Did he get a good mark?"

"I don't know," Ryan said. "He handed it in today. He'll get a better mark than I would."

"Did you fix his bike tire?"

"What is this, Kate?"

It was a fair question. So I took a breath and put it out there. "I want to stay here," I said. "I don't want to go back to my hotel room. I needed some space to think about things, and now I have. I want to come back if you'll have me. But I don't want to be the nanny anymore."

"You don't?"

"No. I don't want to live downstairs anymore and be the help. I want to live up here with you." I blinked hard, because the tears were coming again and my vision was blurring. "I want this life with you. I want to be Dylan's stepmother and sleep with you every night. And it's... it's a lot to want. It's the biggest thing I've ever wanted. I've always tried for small things, things that aren't very hard. But this is hard, and it matters so much. Our timing is always off and everything is complicated, and you might say no. And that terrifies me."

There was a beat of silence. "And that's why you left?"

"Yes," I said. "I was going to tell you everything, and then Amber showed up and—"

Ryan groaned. "For fuck's sake, Kate. Do not tell me you thought I did something with Amber. Do not."

"You were out so late," I said. "My confidence was low."

"I was out late because talking to her messed me up," Ryan said. "I was pissed and I was terrified. I thought I'd drive around for a while, just to clear my head."

I ran a hand through my hair. *This is hard for him,* Tara had said. *Harder than it is for you.* I couldn't blame him for staying out, since I'd left for the same reasons, to get out of the house and clear my thoughts. "Did you?" I asked him. "Clear your head?"

"In a way," Ryan said. "I wanted to score pills, so instead I ended up at a late-night AA meeting. Did you know there are AA meetings downtown? I didn't know it until the other night, when I went to one. I'm not an alcoholic, but no one made me say a fucking thing. I just sat there and listened to those people talk until I didn't want to take pills anymore. Then I drove around for a while. Then I went home."

I sighed. He was so messed up, my Ryan, but at the same time he was so impossibly fucking brave. "I love you," I said.

"Don't mess with me, Kate." His voice was low and choked. "I mean it. Don't say these things if you don't mean them. Because I can't handle it. I just can't."

"I do love you," I said. "I'm crazy about you. Amber made a pass at you, didn't she?"

"She talked about her yoni," Ryan said. "It was fucking awful. I wish I could bleach my brain. You're the only woman I want."

I leaned forward and put my forehead on my knees, the phone still to my ear. "Are you sure?"

"Kate, I've been gone for you for months. I can't remember not being gone for you. You don't even have to do anything. You just have to be. I was stupid five years ago—I was still a kid. But now I've grown up and I've figured a few things out. You're the woman for me. If you come or you go, you're still her. If you leave, it's over for me. You're the only woman I've ever loved in my life, and I don't plan to love any others. So I'm done."

He was saying yes. Yes to everything I wanted. I took a breath and sat straight again. "I'm not leaving. I'm staying here. So now what do we do?"

"You hang up the phone."

"Why?"

"Because I'm outside. You didn't think I was somewhere else, did you?" There was a click, and he hung up.

The front door opened, and Ryan came in. He was wearing jeans, Timberlands, a long-sleeved dark plaid shirt. His dark hair was mussed and he had scruff on his jaw. His expression was set, his gaze intense. He strode toward me as I stood up.

I thought he'd kiss me, maybe grab me and sweep me up, but instead he grabbed my hand and moved past me up the stairs, tugging me after him.

"Where are we going?" I asked.

"To bed," he said.

Really, there wasn't much else to say. And what's a girl to do? So I followed him.

TWENTY-SEVEN

Ryan

I HAD TO HAVE HER. I had to. It was crude, but then again that's what I am. Ryan Riggs, the crude bad boy player. You mess with me, you get dirty.

And if you're Kate, you get everything.

I don't even remember how we got to my bedroom. Half of my clothes were off by the time we got there, and Kate was pulling her sexy jeans off. I caught her by the waist halfway through the act, tossed her on the bed, and yanked them off myself.

I knelt at the edge of the bed and pulled her toward me. She made an "Oh" sound as she realized what I was doing, and then I pushed her panties aside and put my mouth on her.

She cried out, her hips bucking off the bed. I kept going, pausing only long enough to rip her panties down and off of her so I could get full access and kiss her deeper. She tasted insanely good, clean and sweet and perfect, and I knew exactly what she liked. I tongue-kissed her slow and deep, and she went crazy. She grabbed my hair and cursed, but she didn't stop me.

I was pushing her hard, and she begged me to go harder. I spread her wide, used my fingers, and felt her body tense. Maybe she felt as desperate as I did, but I didn't think it was possible. Kate wasn't mine until I *made* her mine, and this time I was going to get what I wanted.

It didn't take her long. It never did when I did this to her. She came hard against my mouth, letting go, making noise. It was fucking divine. I cupped her with my fingers and moved my mouth over her belly, its soft perfect skin, the hard bone of her hip. As she went limp and panting, I kissed my way up her gorgeous fucking body, the line of her ribs. She pulled her bra off and threw it away as I moved up to her breasts and sucked a nipple into my mouth.

Kate moaned, and then she put her hands in my hair again. She pulled me up to her mouth and kissed me. I opened her mouth and licked into it and she went molten, sucking on my tongue. She pushed me over and wrapped her legs around me and the next thing I knew I was sitting on the edge of the bed, hard as iron, my shirt off and my jeans and boxer briefs shoved halfway down my thighs, a glorious, perfectly naked Kate in my lap, wrapped around me.

I cupped her ass, then ran my hands up her bare back. I was fucking nuts for this woman. I buried my face in the side of her neck, feeling her soft red curls brush my skin as I inhaled her and everything went away. My shoulder didn't hurt. There was just me and Kate and this bedroom and the sky outside the window, graying with cold rain. There was just the feeling of her warm skin under my hands and the knowledge that she wasn't leaving.

"I love you," I said against her skin.

She made a sound that was half sigh, half groan. "Don't say something like that after what you just did. It's too much."

"I do," I said.

"I love you, too." She squirmed against me, hot and wet against my cock. "We'll talk more later."

I laughed softly, but I stopped laughing when she moved again and every nerve ending jumped from my cock all the way up my body. "I'll get a condom," I said.

"I'm on the pill," Kate said.

I pulled back and looked at her. Her hair was mussed, her lips reddened, and there were her big, dark, beautiful eyes, looking right at me with honesty.

"You want to?" I asked her.

"Yes," she said.

Condoms were a rule. I mean—they were a very strict fucking rule. It didn't matter who she was, what she said, how hot she was, or what mood I was in. Condoms every time, no exceptions.

But this was Kate. I could be bare *with Kate*. The idea made the blood pound in my head, made my body go hard with want.

At the same time, my heart pounded with fear. Because a mistake, I knew, had far-reaching consequences. Life-altering ones.

"You didn't ask if I'm clean," I said to her.

She traced a fingertip along my lower lip, as if she was memorizing me. "Okay," she said. "Are you clean?"

"Yes." Of course I was fucking clean.

"So am I."

I put an arm around her waist, moved her down so she rubbed my bare cock. I watched her eyelids drift close and her jaw go slack. "Oh, my God," she said.

I lifted my hips and rubbed her, the sensations on my cock almost unbearable. I could feel every hot, slick fold of her.

This was right, I realized. This was the way we were

supposed to be, Kate and me. I was going to marry her and give her as many babies as she wanted anyway. There was no reason to put it off.

I rubbed her again, and her knees pushed wider over my hips, her hips moving under my arm. And then I was inside her, first the head of my cock and then the rest of it as I eased in. The world stopped moving and there was nothing but that, Kate's incredible body squeezing me.

Her eyes closed and her head dropped back, her hair trailing down her back. I moved out and then in again, watching her. "You like that?" I asked her, because I always liked hearing it.

"Yes. Yes. Oh, God, yes." She was practically praying, and I knew I was doing it right. I kept it up, trying to please her, trying not to come as the sensations hit me like body blows. I had never felt anything even close to this. There was no woman in the world like this one.

I moved my hand down between us, brushed her clit, and she said "Oh," her hips moving harder. We were in sync, both of us moving, my hand rubbing, the bed squeaking softly. It took balance and control, but I had both. My only goals in life were to keep her right where I had her, and to make her come.

Kate bit her lip and her knees clamped me hard. Then she came, her body bucking, her inner muscles rippling and squeezing me. I pushed her back on the bed, rolling on top of her, and I came too, my hands digging into her skin, my cock deep inside her. It felt hot and dirty and sacred.

Only her. Only me.

Ryan Riggs, the player, was officially done. And I didn't even miss him.

TWENTY-EIGHT

Kate

WE HAD time until Dylan needed to be picked up from school, so we lay in bed and talked. Ryan had no problem sprawling naked on his back with his arm crooked behind his head, but I made him pull the sheet up over him because naked Ryan was distracting. There was no way to talk when he looked like that.

I lay next to him as the cold spits of rain hit the window, curled on my side, my chin on his shoulder. We talked about me moving upstairs and whether to hire another nanny. We talked about the future. I told him my business idea, and he was fully behind it. We talked about Riggs Auto, Riggs Auto Two, and working with Dex. He told me about the conversation with Amber, that it had been a test to see if she could get close to Dylan. Ryan told her to talk to his lawyer, but his lawyer hadn't received anything yet.

"So she might sue for custody," I said.

He shifted, the muscles in his shoulder flexing under my chin. "Maybe. Or maybe she'll take off again."

"But she'll be back. Someday."

He was quiet for a second. "Yes. Probably she will."

"She's going to hurt Dylan. A mother who comes and goes from your life, without really caring about you, would hurt anyone."

"If it happens, we deal with it," Ryan said. "He has me, and that's legal. He has us."

He has us. This was really happening, Ryan and me. We were all in. And I didn't feel scared. I felt excited, hopeful for the future. It wasn't so bad, facing challenges when you had someone you loved at your side.

"We need to tell Dylan about us," I said. "Today."

"You know, I actually think he'll be okay with it," Ryan said. "He's been miserable without you. I think he loves you."

I smiled against his warm skin. "You think so?"

"You'd have to ask him. But yes, I think so." He moved under my chin, leaned over and picked up his cell phone, checked the time. "Which reminds me, he gets out of school in twenty minutes."

"I'll go get him," I said, sitting up and looking for my clothes.

"I'll do it." Ryan scrubbed a hand through his hair. There was nothing more gorgeous on this planet than Ryan Riggs lazing in bed, a sheet barely covering him, showing all those miles of skin and muscle and stubble and tousled hair. "You go back to your hotel and check out."

"I'll trade you," I said. I picked the hotel key out of my purse and tossed it to him. "You go check me out. I'm going to go see Dylan."

HE LOOKED SO SMALL, carried along in the crowd of kids coming out of the school. I was in the pickup lane in a long line of cars, everyone waiting for their kid. For the first time, I wondered quietly to myself if I would ever be able to start thinking of Dylan as mine. In a way, I already did. But we would take that one day at a time.

I spotted him almost right away, even though he was wearing a coat with the hood up in the rain. I knew that coat, the set of his shoulders, the way he walked. I recognized his jeans, because they were almost too short—he was growing like a weed. I recognized the tuft of hair that peeked from under his hood.

I was out of the car and standing on the pavement before I even realized I'd moved. I pushed my own hood back and waved at him.

Dylan paused when he saw me. I saw now that his face was pale and anxious. This was a hard week for him. The adults in his life were all acting like idiots, and he didn't know what was going on or what was going to happen next. Well, all of that ended now.

I waved at him again and smiled. He came toward me, and the look of hope that he so obviously tried to keep down ripped my heart out. When he got close enough, I bent down and scooped him up in a big bear hug, right in front of everyone. I lifted him straight off the ground.

Dylan hugged me back. He was getting heavy, but he was still a kid.

"Kate," he said after a minute, "are you back?"

I squeezed my boy tighter. "Yes," I said. "I am."

TWENTY-NINE

Ryan

One month later

SINCE WE'D NEVER HAD a wedding in the Riggs family before, we improvised a lot of things. We held it in the backyard of the Riggs house on a dark, cloudy day on Thanksgiving weekend, with cold wind and snow threatening to fly. The women wore matching dark brown knitted shawls over their shoulders, and those of us in suits just suffered the cold. There were about forty guests, all from Emily's side: her parents, women who worked at the salon, a couple of cousins, some cops who worked for Emily's mother and had known her all her life. Luke had Dex, Jace, and me, and Dex was late.

Emily's sister Lauren was late too, because she was the one who had gone to the guest house to make sure Dex got ready. Maybe I was the only one who noticed that it took them a long time, but then again maybe I wasn't. Emily stared daggers at her sister when she finally showed up to the house, and Kate caught my eye, eloquently lifting an eyebrow.

She looked gorgeous in her dark green dress. Of course she looked fucking gorgeous—she was Kate. The dress curved over her perfect tits, then tucked in just below them before draping to the ground. It matched her dark red curls, which she wore down over her shoulders. I'd helped her get ready, and I'd behaved like a gentleman, but I wasn't going to be a gentleman later, when I got that dress off her. No fucking way.

Dylan was in a suit and tie that we'd carefully picked out for him, waiting for his serious gig as the ring-bearer. He didn't care about the cold. He was happy just to be here and to be a part of the action.

Dylan, like I'd predicted, had taken pretty well to Kate becoming my girlfriend. We kept his routine steady: Kate took him to school and back while I worked at Riggs Auto Two, and I took over evenings and weekends while Kate went to class and studied. Amber had gone back to Thailand, thank fucking God. I hoped it was for good, but somehow I doubted it. In the meantime, she was completely gone from my mind.

Along with school, Kate was in the process of starting her business. It was going to be a tutoring school, aimed especially at helping kids with learning disabilities keep up with their schoolwork. With Lauren's help, Kate was going to rent the space, hire tutors, and run it while she trained to be a teacher herself. Then she was going to take over a lot of the teaching duties, which was what she really wanted to do. There was nothing exactly like it in Westlake, it was going to be amazing, and Kate was going for it.

I'd never seen her so happy, and whatever made Kate happy was fine with me. She'd taken over the basement apartment as her office and study room, which meant she spent a lot of time down there.

But every night she left the basement and came to bed with me.

We tried to be quiet. We really did. But on the nights when Dylan had a sleepover, we made a lot of fucking noise.

Riggs Auto Two was making good money. The pain in my shoulder had mostly cleared up, which meant I could work longer hours. Dex was hung over half the time, but the man could fix cars like nobody's business. He wasn't an oil-change guy; he liked hard problems, obscure makes and models, impossible-to-find parts. And, it turned out, so did I. If you had a classic car that needed an overhaul, Dex and I were your men. We could spend days on a single car, tossing problems and solutions back and forth, making it work again. After all these years, we actually had something we could talk about without killing each other. The word was slowly getting out, and we were getting more inquiries for custom jobs. The custom jobs were fewer, but they paid more.

It was time for the ceremony to start, so we left the house where we'd been eating and drinking and filed out into the yard while the guests took their seats. I didn't mind that it was under a gray sky; there was something fitting about it, about doing this on Thanksgiving when everyone else was eating dinner with families. The Riggs brothers had never had a family. Today seemed like a good day to start building one.

"Welcome to the party, man," I said to Dex as he slid into the best man's spot beside me at the front next to the altar. "Nice of you to show up."

"Fuck off, Riggs," Dex said. He was actually cleaned up: showered, hair combed, shaved for once. His suit fit and his tie was straight. Since Lauren had taken so long getting him ready in the guest house, I had to assume she should get all the credit. Jace took his spot next to me, and I had to do a double-take. My tattooed ex-con little brother cleaned up pretty good, too.

Jace caught my eye. "I know," he said, looking me up and down. "This is fucking weird."

"We are never wearing suits again," Dex said quietly and definitively as the music started. "Not for anyone, ever."

"What if I marry Tara?" Jace said. "No, forget it. I'm not inviting either of you if I marry Tara."

"I'm keeping mine," I said. I was going to need it, because I planned to marry Kate as soon as she would let me. I didn't know if she knew that yet. I caught her eye as she stood on the other side of the altar with the other bridesmaids. She looked back at me and her cheeks flushed. Maybe she was thinking the same thing.

Dylan came out on cue and stood by the altar. Luke came out, looking pretty fucking good, and waited. The music changed and Emily came down our makeshift aisle, on the arm of her dad. She looked spectacular and happy. Everyone sighed. I could kind of see why people liked weddings so much.

Emily and Luke joined hands, and the justice of the peace they'd brought to officiate started talking. It was going to be kept to a short ceremony so everyone wouldn't get too cold before going back into the house to drink some more. Dylan only fidgeted a little bit before being asked to present the rings.

Toward the end, I looked at Dex and noticed he wasn't even watching the ceremony. He was standing in place next to the altar, but his gaze was fixed on Lauren Parker, a few feet away on the other side of the altar in the maid of honor spot. And she was looking at him, the two of them so focused on each other that nothing else existed. They were doing a full-on staring contest. Lauren's eyes were narrowed, like she was pissed at him and she wanted him to know it. Dex's expression was impossible to read, but there was a gleam in his eye that was a little bit gleeful, like he'd won something. What the fuck was going on?

Dex and Lauren, I thought. *Never gonna happen. No fucking way.*

I moved my gaze back to Kate and watched her for the rest of the ceremony. It finished, Luke and Emily kissed, and everyone clapped. Then the music started again and we all started to move toward the house.

Kate came over to me and took my hand. "Come here, Bad Boy of Baseball," she said.

"Where are we going?"

"Follow me."

She led me away from the others and around the side of the house, where we were alone. Then she pinned me against the wall and kissed me.

I was all in. Her arms around my neck, my hands on her waist, I kissed her back until she broke away. "What was that for?" I asked.

"For looking gorgeous in a suit," she said.

"You already knew that."

"I'm freshly reminded of it. It was also for looking at me like that during the wedding. And for being wonderful. And for being all mine."

"Okay," I said, brushing a curl from her cheek. "I'll cop to those things." I pulled her to me and kissed her again. "How long do we have to stick around here?" I asked when I finished.

She leaned in to me. It was cold, and I kept my arms tight around her, keeping her warm. "Do you think they'll notice if we leave now?" she asked.

I smiled at her. I had no idea what I had ever done without this woman. "I give Dylan five minutes before he comes around that corner, asking what we're doing," I said.

Kate leaned up and brushed her lips against mine. "Five minutes then, Ryan," she said. "Let's see if we can make it count."

ALSO BY JULIE KRISS

The Riggs Brothers Series

Drive Me Wild

Take Me Down

Work Me Up

Make Me Beg

The Bad Billionaire Series

Bad Billionaire

Dirty Sweet Wild

Rich Dirty Dangerous

Back in Black

Standalone

Spite Club

The Eden Hills Duet

Bad Boyfriend

Bad Wedding

93617945R00118

Made in the USA
Middletown, DE
15 October 2018